SUGAR TYCOON

SUGAR DADDIES #4

CHARITY PARKERSON

--Warning: This book is intended for readers over the age of 18.

Copyright © 2018 Charity Parkerson
Editor: Vicky Reese
ISBN-13: 978-1-946099-36-5
ISBN-10: 1-946099-36-8

INTRODUCTION

Wyld West is the billionaire playboy who's as eccentric as his name. Not only has he never been in love, Wyld doesn't believe it exists. Until an angelic younger man comes to his rescue and nothing makes sense any longer.

While delivering meals to the homeless, Micah stumbles upon Wyld, bleeding and in need of help. Two months later, he's still finding ways to see Wyld. The man is caustic and unlikable. In fact, everyone constantly warns Micah against a friendship with Wyld, but all Micah sees is someone as lonely as him.

When Wyld makes Micah a crazy and unexpected

offer, it'll be them against the world. Micah will have his work cut out for him if he hopes to keep his family, friends, and his sugar tycoon. Luckily, Micah is a fighter. Now, if only everyone else would cooperate.

ONE

LIKE MOST PEOPLE, Wyld wasn't immune to seeing a couple newly married and in love. Fortunately, he'd missed the actual wedding, leaving him free to enjoy the open bar of the wedding reception. The two grooms were missing. Wyld had shamelessly helped them sneak away earlier. Now, he was left with nothing better to do than get plastered while people watching in the hot California sun. Well, person watching. There was only one face in the crowd Wyld cared to see—Micah.

There was so much more to Micah than met the eye, but damn he was easy to look at. Two months earlier, one of the grooms of this shindig had punched Wyld in the face before leaving him bleeding in an alley. Then, Micah, the angel of miracles had found him. From the first time Wyld set eyes upon Micah, he'd been struck stupid. Micah was way too young for Wyld. Still, Wyld found every excuse to be wherever Micah was, inserting himself in the man's life.

As Wyld looked on, Micah tossed his head back and laughed. Even his blond curls bounced with youth. Wyld threw back another shot of whisky. Another face caught his attention, Detroit Amherst. Micah's date for the day. Damn. That thought alone had Wyld ordering another shot to rinse the bad taste from his mouth. According to Micah, Detroit was just a friend. Wyld hoped like hell that was true. Not because he had every intention of corrupting the angel, but because of Detroit. Nobody deserved that guy. Wide-shouldered, brown haired and blue eyed, Detroit looked exactly like a comic book hero complete with the split curl haircut. Unlike the superhero, Detroit was a player. Women and men alike flocked to Detroit, and he accepted all takers. As far as Wyld could tell, he didn't have a genuine bone in his body. People probably said the same of Wyld. That knowledge didn't stop his distaste for Detroit, especially since for someone who was supposed to be there with Micah, Detroit seemed to be on the make.

Wyld didn't look a gift distraction in the mouth. With Detroit otherwise engaged, Wyld headed Micah's way. For a moment, their gazes met. It was like a punch to the chest every time. Micah's eyes flashed with happiness—as if he'd spotted a friend, before someone else pulled Micah's attention away. Wyld picked up the pace, going after his prey. No one stopped him to talk. People rarely did unless they wanted something from him. Today, that was a good thing. He couldn't let Micah get away. Detroit wasn't likely to let Wyld have too much time with Micah. As much as Detroit obviously didn't want the boy, it was equally obvious he wanted no one else to have him. That was especially true of Wyld. He might have a point there. Wyld wasn't a good person, nor did he care to be. But there was something about Micah. He was different.

⸻

Two months. That's how long Micah had known the real estate tycoon named Wyld West. For someone whose life was somewhat boring, meeting a guy like Wyld was a never-ending roller coaster.

Complete with adrenaline rushes and sudden drops. Since he'd found Wyld, bleeding in the alley behind the Den of Payne—a members only sex club—Micah shouldn't have been surprised the guy had a few issues. Yet, Wyld still shocked him daily. Today was no different.

"You know, I secured an invitation to this just to see you."

Micah kept his face averted as Wyld's delicious British accent caressed his ear. He couldn't let the man see him smile. Micah knew from experience, Wyld wouldn't stop if he got the reaction he sought.

After rearranging his features to seem unaffected, Micah turned and met the sexiest whiskey-colored eyes. "That's kind of crass, don't you think? Crashing a wedding reception just to stalk a teenage boy." He was nineteen and legal, but Micah loved teasing Wyld.

As he'd expected, Wyld's expression turned even more devilish than usual. "Mhmm, yes. I'm a dirty scoundrel."

Micah couldn't stop smiling. It had only taken him a quick internet search to learn Wyld was thirty-five. He'd also learned Wyld had been born near the Cheshire area to parents who were described as "nouveau riche" for earning their money rather than inheriting. In an interview with an affluent magazine, Wyld had credited his American born father for teaching him the art of property investment. He'd turned a three-million-dollar university graduation gift from his parents into a billion-dollar business. Now, he was one of the youngest billionaires in the world. Micah didn't care about any of that—not the man's age or money. He liked Wyld's dry wit and wicked sense of humor. No one was inappropriate with Micah. Being with Wyld was like throwing off the chains he usually wore.

"I'm sure you have someone willing to spank you on speed dial."

"Shhh," Wyld said with a laugh. He half-heartedly tried covering Micah's mouth. "You're too young for that filth."

Micah swatted his hand away. "You started it."

Wyld snagged Micah's hand and brought it to his lips. "Let's sneak away."

The eye roll was out of his control, but Micah felt it all the way to his soul. Wyld never took anything seriously. He pulled his hand away from Wyld's lips. "This is Hendrix and Jude's wedding reception. We can't sneak away."

"I don't see why not. Jude and Hendrix ran while no one was watching over half an hour ago."

At Wyld's claim, Micah turned in a circle, eyeing the crowd. Since Jude stood close to six-five, he should've been easy to spot if he was there. He wasn't. "Oh, ha. Still," Micah said, focusing on Wyld once more. "I came with Detroit. It wouldn't be right for me to run out on him."

Jude's mother, Viv appeared at Wyld's side. Her long silver hair hung in a braid over one shoulder. "Have either of you seen Jude?" she asked. Her light gray gaze swept the crowd.

Wyld's gaze never wavered from Micah. His mouth lifted in one corner in the world's wickedest smirk as he motioned toward the house. "He came through here, headed in that direction not two minutes ago."

With a distracted pat to Wyld's arm, she headed that way. "Thank you, sweetie."

"About that sneaking away," Wyld said the moment she left them alone. "Detroit seems otherwise engaged. You can text him once we're gone to let him know you've made other arrangements for the day."

Unlike his fruitless hunt for Jude, Micah spotted Detroit right away. His lips were pressed to a blonde woman's ear while his hand rested on her ass. Micah swallowed it down. The way he always did. "What would you like to do?" he asked, focusing on Wyld once more.

No triumph marred Wyld's features, sparing Micah's pride. With a quick glance around, Wyld linked his fingers through Micah's and headed for a back-gate Micah hadn't noticed earlier. It was hidden by a large palm tree. Once they were past the tree and out the gate, a spurt of excitement raced through Micah. He never did anything unexpected.

Wyld led Micah to a red Lotus. The car was as flashy as its owner. After Wyld opened the passenger side door for Micah, Micah slid inside and tried to figure out how to belt himself in, since he'd never dealt with racing seats before. Luckily, he figured it out before Wyld caught him struggling. Micah didn't think Wyld would make fun of his ignorance, but he didn't want to appear completely inept. Once safely strapped in, Micah eyed the inside of the car. It was somewhat plain for a car that cost as much as a small house.

They made it a mile before Micah's phone buzzed with an incoming text. He knew before digging out his phone who it would be. Detroit's name flashed across the screen. Only his inability to make Detroit worry had Micah reading the message.

Detroit: *Where did you disappear to?*

After a moment of considering several lies, Micah decided to go with a half-truth.

Micah: *You were busy hitting on some blonde chick, so I left with a friend. Have fun with your latest victim. I'll catch up with you tomorrow.*

There. Anything else Detroit had to say could wait. Micah powered down his phone before any new messages could roll in and make him feel guilty. With his obligation to Detroit out of the way, Micah eyed the man behind the wheel. He was the only person Micah knew who could pull off dressing eccentric to the extreme. There was a black skull ring on the man's pinky. It had diamonds for eyes. While Wyld's jacket looked halfway normal, except for the fine stripes that actually spelled out the designer's name if a person looked close enough, Wyld wore nothing but suspenders beneath. The man's hard, tan chest peeked out beneath the lapels. The sight made Micah smile. He honestly didn't know what it was about Wyld. Just being in the man's presence made Micah happy.

A curl fell across Wyld's eye when he turned his head, catching Micah staring. He winked before going back to watching the road. It occurred to Micah, he'd left with Wyld without a single clue or care as to where they were headed. They didn't go far before Wyld turned into the parking lot of a playground. Micah knew it well. A few of the homeless he visited each week stayed nearby.

"We're going to a park?" Micah asked, rhetorically.

Still, Wyld answered. "Yes. Isn't this where children go for play dates, my child?"

Micah's eyebrows rose. He didn't know whether to laugh or be insulted. "I imagine you'd know better than me."

Wyld parked before looking his way. "I do love a good sturdy swing," Wyld said. He popped his sunglasses on before slipping from the car. Wyld circled the vehicle and opened Micah's door. Even he didn't understand why he sat there and waited for it to happen. It wasn't as if he was used to being treated in such a way. Once again, there was just something about Wyld. Micah was always holding his breath, waiting for the man to make the next move, and set Micah free.

<hr />

Wyld headed for the tire swings with an obviously confused and reluctant Micah on his heels. He leapt onto the first tire and set it in motion.

Thankfully, the place was dead. Wyld wanted Micah to himself. Micah sat on the edge of the tire beside him, looking unsure of the equipment. He eyed the swing Wyld occupied.

"How much did your suit cost?"

Wyld glance down at himself. "No idea. Why?"

Micah's smile was everything. "Because I imagine I would choke over the price. Yet, you just jumped on the first dirt covered swing you came to."

"Let's be honest, I'll probably never wear it again." Wyld settled deeper into the huge tire where he could relax and stare at Micah. "You should join in the fun. When was the last time you played?"

"I don't know," Micah said. He set a foot on the edge of Wyld's tire and pushed, keeping him moving in a gentle rocking motion. He looked content.

Wyld couldn't stop staring. "You're a nurturer, aren't you?"

Micah's smile was back. "I suppose I am. When I know other people are happy and comfortable, it makes me happy."

"Whoever you're dating is a lucky bastard." Wyld couldn't have stopped the claim if he tried. He hadn't been this interested in anyone in... ever.

"I'm not dating anyone."

That was good news for Wyld. Not that he

intended to show his hand. "That's a travesty. Why are you single?"

"Why are you?" Micah countered, making Wyld bite back a laugh. He loved when the boy turned defiant. His eyes flashed with fire.

That's exactly why Wyld didn't back down. "I'm rude, spoiled, caustic, and drink too much. Not to mention, I spend a great deal of time and money in sex clubs, getting high on every vice imaginable. No one could love me. What's your excuse?"

"I'm only sexually aroused by people I feel a deep connection with, which drives men away, and leaves me deeply frustrated."

Wyld blinked. Never in a million years had he expected that candid answer, especially falling from such sweet lips. Before Wyld could dredge up a response, Micah continued the confessions.

"If I meet someone I like, by the time they turn me on, they only see me as a friend any longer, compounding the problem. I'm permanently in everyone's friend zone."

"Do you have someone you want?"

Micah surprised him by not once backing down. "Yes, but he doesn't want me."

"That doesn't surprise me."

Micah winced.

"Your generation is plagued with idiots," Wyld explained, because he couldn't let Micah misunderstand. "How can I help?"

Micah's dimples made an appearance. "You can't make someone want me who doesn't want me."

"You'd be surprised what I can do. So, tell me why you think this idiot doesn't want you."

"I'm me and he's him," Micah said, his gaze skirting away.

Wyld's eye roll physically hurt. "Detroit. I should've known."

The way Micah's eyes flashed with humor had Wyld fighting his dark nature. "You really don't like Detroit, do you?"

"No." Wyld didn't bother sugar coating things.

"Why?"

Wyld held Micah's stare. "I suppose he reminds me a lot of myself, and I hate me. So, why should he be spared my loathing?"

Micah's smile disappeared making Wyld wish he hadn't been honest. "It doesn't matter if you like you, because I like you." He was serious. It was in his every word.

The longer they spoke, the closer Wyld felt himself leaning toward Micah, trying to soak up the boy's kindness. "That's because you hold a distinction no one else can claim, I'm nice to you. Also, you're a fool."

Instead of being insulted, Micah laughed. "I know. Everyone tells me daily."

Wyld ate up Micah's good humor, even as his mood deteriorated. "That's why I like you. You're honest, even with yourself. But the next time someone calls you a fool, I expect you to punch them in the dick, or we can't be friends anymore."

With a shake of his head, Micah straightened away, obviously noticing how close he'd let Wyld get. "You're the strangest person I've ever met. I don't know why I can't stay away."

"Because I'm incorrigible, and you love it."

"Maybe. What would you like to do next?"

Wyld fought his way out of the swing and held his hand out for Micah. "Since we got all dressed up for the day, I'm taking you out." Micah's happy-sounding laughter drove Wyld wild. "First, we'll go to dinner and then dancing. Afterward, I'll let you choose between coming home with me or hopping a flight to Hawaii."

A snort sounded behind him as Wyld dragged Micah toward the car. "You're ridiculous. Normal people don't hop a flight to Hawaii—zero planning."

Wyld opened the passenger side door for Micah.

"I'm not normal, Angel. The faster you accept that, the less frustrated you'll be by me."

"I'm not frustrated by you," Micah said as Wyld closed the door.

Wyld's smirk was out of his control as he circled the car. He was about to corrupt the hell out of an angel. The boy just didn't know it yet.

———

It didn't take Micah long to realize Wyld said a lot of things in a joking tone that he was one hundred percent serious about. Dinner in itself had been an adventure. Micah had never been fawned over the way the staff of the high-class restaurant tripped over themselves to please him and Wyld. It seemed Wyld was a regular and known for his tipping generosity.

From there, they'd gone to a members' only dance club where—once again—everyone had been at Wyld's disposal. Countless men, gorgeous men, had tried speaking to Wyld. He'd ignored every single one, speaking only to Micah. Micah was left breathless from not only the nonstop dancing, but the way Wyld's gaze never seemed to waver from him.

The later the night got, the slower the songs turned and the lower the lights became. Before Micah realized what was happening, he was in Wyld's arms. His face hurt from smiling. Wyld's jacket had disappeared two hours earlier, leaving him shirtless. Micah couldn't stop touching the man's bare skin. If Wyld noticed, he didn't call Micah on it. Instead, he held Micah closer.

"So, angel of miracles, what'll it be? My place or Hawaii?"

A chuckle that sounded exhausted even to Micah escaped him. "I can't go to Hawaii. There are people expecting meals tomorrow."

"My place it is," Wyld said against his ear.

Micah's heart skipped a beat. He'd already warned Wyld about his issues with sex. Micah liked Wyld. A lot. But they didn't know each other well enough for Micah to feel comfortable enough for sex. Pushing things would only lead to hard feelings. Micah knew. He'd been there. The thing was, Micah was also about ninety-eight percent certain that Wyld only saw him as a friend—like all men. "What do you think will happen back at your place?"

Wyld stroked the small of Micah's back. "First, I think you'll drive me home, because I've been drinking. Then, I think you'll stay because you're too nice to leave me alone, and knowing me, I'll keep drinking until I pass out. Finally, we'll talk until I fall asleep and you'll consider calling a cab to take you home. In the end, you'll decide to stay because you won't be able to help yourself."

That sounded about right to Micah. "Sounds like my typical night out." Even Micah heard the disappointment in his voice. He knew he shouldn't expect more. In truth, he didn't know what he wanted. But Wyld was different from everyone. He made Micah's skin feel too tight and his heart beat a little faster. So, naturally, Wyld wouldn't feel the same.

Wyld leaned away. His gaze moved over Micah's face, seeing too much. His expression turned serious. Micah didn't want Wyld to see his heart. He pasted on his brightest smile.

"I'm ridiculously excited to drive your car."

"It's yours."

Micah's smile fell. "What?"

Wyld's somber expression never wavered. "If you like it, it's yours. On one condition—never turn fake on me like that again."

A genuine laugh rose inside Micah. "You can't give me a car."

"I can do whatever the fuck I want. I'm me. Not

to mention, I have two more just like it. A yellow one and a blue one. Would you prefer one of those?"

Micah realized Wyld was serious. "You cannot give me a car, Wyld."

Wyld's hands slid from the small of Micah's back to his ass, he hauled Micah closer. Their bodies went flush. Wyld continued swaying to the music even as his expression turned darker by the moment. "You should really stop trying to tell me what I can't do."

The hands on his ass were distracting as hell. Still, Micah searched for an argument. "I can't afford the insurance on a car like that. It's probably best I stay in my lane."

Wyld cupped his jaw and held on. His thumb brushed Micah's bottom lip. His gaze locked on the motion as if fascinated by the sight of his hand on Micah's skin. "You're my only friend. I want to spoil you."

Micah covered Wyld's hand with his, bringing Wyld's gaze back to his. He waited until he had Wyld's attention before speaking. "You don't have to spoil me to be my friend. When we met, I didn't know who you were, and I still wanted to be with you. Nothing has changed. If you lost everything tomorrow, still nothing would change. Okay?"

Wyld's intensity didn't lessen. "I'll buy you a car

with affordable insurance. Or," he said, brightening. "Just hear me out, I could add you to my policy, and then you could share all my cars."

Micah took a breath and shook his head. Wyld was impossible. It was his most endearing trait. Micah toyed with Wyld's suspenders, sneaking touches of his chest. "Exactly how many cars do you have?"

Wyld shrugged. "I've never counted." Wyld's fingers found the buttons of Micah's shirt. He felt the material loosen beneath the man's touch. Once the two halves fell open, Wyld shoved his hands beneath and drew Micah closer once more. Micah bit back a gasp when their bare skin met. Wyld's body moved in time with the music. A fine sheen of sweat coated his skin. The flashing lights made him feel like he was in a dream. "So, about Hawaii..."

Something between a laugh and a groan escaped Micah. He didn't know how to deal with someone like Wyld. Someone who always got their way. He didn't know how to deny Wyld. Micah also wasn't sure he ever wanted to tell the man no. One day soon that would bite him in the ass. The way it always did when he gave too much of himself.

TWO

"WHERE DID YOU GO YESTERDAY?"

Micah tried looking every which way but Detroit's. "Nowhere special. Just down the road."

"If you were ready to leave, you could've said something. I would've taken you home."

"I didn't want to go home," Micah said, trying to keep things vague. "Besides, you looked busy with some blonde."

Detroit shrugged. His large tanned shoulders caught the sunlight, drawing Micah's gaze. Detroit was like a beautiful piece of art. People couldn't help but stare. "You know me. I was just killing time. I'm never too busy for you."

That was true. Detroit always made time for him. The knowledge had Micah feeling twice as guilty. He didn't keep secrets from Detroit. They were friends. Like now, he knew there were a million and one things Detroit would rather be doing than helping him deliver meals, but he still showed up.

Micah chewed his bottom lip as he picked his way through the alley, keeping an eye out for Driver, one of his regulars. "I left with Wyld." The words were out there before he could stop them. Micah needed someone to talk to. His excitement ran too deep.

Detroit shifted the bag filled with food boxes from one hand to the other. His expression spoke volumes. He thought Micah was a dumbass. "You left with Wyld."

Despite Detroit's dry tone, Micah couldn't reel his happiness back in. "We had the best time, Detroit. We went to the park."

"A park."

Micah didn't know, nor did he care why Detroit kept repeating everything he said. "Yes. I haven't been in years. Then, he took me to dinner at some place right on the beach. It was amazing. Oh, and then we went dancing. I haven't had that much fun in... ever, I guess."

"Your happiness is evident, but I don't know where to start."

"What's that supposed to mean?" As the words left his lips, he spotted Driver dipping through a hole in the alley's fence. "Oh, there's Driver. Driver."

At his shout, the dark-haired man turned. A bright smile lit the man's dirt-covered and tanned face. "Hey, Micah." His gaze slid Detroit's way, but as always, Driver dismissed him. A few of the people he helped were like that. Micah didn't know why. "I wondered if I would see you today, since you're out of school for the summer."

Micah's face hurt from smiling. Between his night with Wyld and doing what he loved, he couldn't be happier. "You know I would never leave you hanging."

"You should," Driver said. His expression turned serious. The man's light blue gaze never wavered from Micah. "You only live once, Micah. Get out and do something besides digging around in the dirt with people like me. See the world."

Detroit reached past Micah, passing over a tray of food.

Even though Driver accepted, his gaze never wavered from Micah. "You don't intend to listen to me, do you?" he asked, going back to smiling.

Without a care for the dirt covering his clothes,

Micah patted his shoulder. "I'm listening, but you'd be surprised how much of the world I've seen."

"Then for fuck's sake." Driver swiped his fingers over his mouth. "Sorry, sweetheart. I shouldn't talk like that in front of you."

Micah bit back a smile.

Driver started over. "You should at least take a vacation. All of us will still be here when you get back, begging for a handout."

His words stabbed Micah through the heart. Driver was one of the many veterans he visited each week. It broke him that Driver lived in the streets. The man wasn't all that much older than Micah, but his eyes said he'd seen things he'd never forget. "You shouldn't have to beg. I wish you would go to the mission and let them help you." Even Micah heard the desperation in his voice. He wanted to do more but didn't know how or have the means to help.

"They won't let me take my dog," Driver reminded him. "I can't leave Sam."

Each time Micah saw Driver, he made the same claim. Micah had never seen this dog. He wasn't sure it was real. He pasted on an understanding smile. "Speaking of Sam, I brought an extra box of food for him. Just don't tell on me, okay?" Micah dug out the food and passed it over. Driver's smile made everything worthwhile. The food he fixed for what might be an imaginary dog came from Micah's fridge. "It's not much, but I'm a poor college student."

Driver dropped his gaze to the ground. "I think you're an angel in disguise."

A soft chuckle escaped Micah. "Nah. I just like you better than most. Don't tell on me for that one either."

The man's smile reappeared. He met Micah's stare again. "Thank you." He gave Detroit a quick nod too before disappearing through the hole in the fence.

Micah's chest ached as he watched the man go. Some days he felt so small and helpless. "Is it just me, or did he seem sadder than usual?" When Detroit didn't respond, Micah glanced behind him. Detroit was staring at him as if waiting for Micah's full attention. "What?"

"You're going to get hurt."

"I seriously doubt Driver would ever hurt me."

"That's not what I'm talking about, and you know it. Wyld West is bad news. He's rich and bored. For now, you're something new for him to play with. When your shine dims in his eyes, he'll move on to the next thing."

Dealing with Detroit the way he always did,

Micah closed the distance between them and hugged him. He squeezed as hard as he could. Sometimes, Micah pretended he could squish the bitterness from Detroit. He didn't know why Detroit had such a jaded view of the world, but Micah wished he could fix it. Micah also wished he knew why it felt like there was something he couldn't see eating away their friendship. It was like they got farther away every day. He kissed Detroit's cheek. Micah leaned away, meeting Detroit's gaze while still clinging to his waist. "Listen to me. I want you to hear me, okay?"

Detroit gave him a sharp nod. "I'm listening."

Since it was important to Micah that Detroit understood him, he didn't hold back. "This is my life. Not once have I lectured you on hopping from one person to the next without a care to anyone's feelings. Do I have thoughts on that? Yes. I have lots and lots of opinions on the way you treat people who trust you with their bodies. But, I keep them to myself. I'm asking you, as my friend, to keep your nose out of this. Okay?"

"I don't know if I can make that promise."

With a growl, Micah took a step back. He was already tired of defending himself. "Give me the rest of the meals. You're free to do whatever." He couldn't look at Detroit. His anger was too deep.

Detroit held tight to the bag. "I'm not leaving you out here by yourself."

"I'm not asking for your permission to go alone. I'm telling you I'm good and get lost."

The way Detroit narrowed his eyes said shit was about to get ugly. "No."

"Look, Detroit, I'm tired of arguing for the day. We haven't had any luck finding the last few people on our list. If you want to help, just take the food boxes back to my house, stuff them in the fridge, and be free. I'm sure Dad is there to let you inside. I'll try delivering the rest tomorrow."

A loud sigh rent the air. Detroit's frustration couldn't be missed. As far as Micah was concerned, it didn't hold a candle to his aggravation. "Again, I'm not leaving you out here alone."

Micah shrugged. "Fine. You can drop me off at the campus bookstore. I want to sell back last year's textbooks that I no longer need."

Detroit nodded. "Fine."

"Fine," Micah agreed. He didn't think it necessary to add, once he'd finished selling back his books, he planned to call Wyld. It was addicting having someone happy to hear from him. Sometimes, it seemed like—somewhere along the line—Detroit had stopped being happy to spend time with him. The idea broke his heart. He didn't know when they'd stopped being friends, but some days, it felt like they had.

WYLD PACED THE FLOOR. SOMETIMES, IT WAS out of his control. He would walk from one end of his house to the other which with seventeen thousand feet, was no small feat. After he'd trailed from one end to the other, he hit the stairs, going from floor to floor. Even though it was only his assistant Cortland and himself living there, he didn't let a single room go bare. Most were bedrooms, in case he ever decided to throw a huge party and let several people stay overnight. There was also a home gym, an observatory, theater room, and collector's gallery. None of it brought him pleasure. Not that he'd ever tried to buy happiness. What would be the point? True bliss didn't exist. Not for people like him.

By the time Wyld made his second round of the third floor, he was plotting ways to find trouble. Idle hands and all that. He'd proven that saying true a thousand times over. His cell phone buzzed in his back pocket, startling him. Wyld fought to pull the device from his pocket and was more than a little aggravated by the time he had it. That is, until he spotted Micah's name.

The ridiculous smile pulling at his lips was out of his control. He pressed the phone to his ear. "Hello, sexy angel. How may I service you?"

"I'm happy to hear your voice too."

At Micah's response, and the sound of his gorgeous voice, Wyld's smile somehow managed to grow brighter. "You always know what I'm really thinking, even when my mouth is stupid."

"There's nothing stupid about your mouth. In fact, it's one of the things I like best about you."

Wyld found the closest bedroom and closed himself inside. He crawled onto the bed and stared at the ceiling. His angel's perfect features filled his mind. Wyld swore he could almost reach out and touch Micah's soft blond curls. That's how clear the man's picture was in Wyld's head. "What can my glorious mouth do for you then?"

A soft chuckle came through the line, caressing his ear. Somehow, Wyld just knew Micah was blushing. "You could tell me what you've been doing today?"

After shifting the phone from one ear to the other, Wyld snuggled deeper into the pillows, and closed his eyes. He felt closer to Micah already. "I've taken twelve thousand five hundred and thirty-six steps today, walking around my house."

"Whoa. I have one of those apps on my phone that tells me how far I've walked, but I never look at it.

"Oh, I didn't use an app," Wyld admitted. "I counted."

Something brushed across the phone as if Micah shifted positions. "Are you bored?"

"Mhmm," Wyld hummed, wondering how honest he should be. In the end, it was Micah, so he told the truth. "There's nothing I haven't done at least a hundred times. I find life rather lacking."

"I doubt there's anything I can add to your life to change that."

Wyld didn't hesitate to argue. "Not true. I get to start over, doing everything like it was the first time as I show it to you. What do you say, Angel? Want to play?"

Micah being Micah, he didn't back down. Wyld had known he wouldn't. "What do you have in mind?"

"When was the last time you talked on the phone all night, telling your every secret?"

"Um, never," Micah said with a laugh. "I don't have many secrets."

"You're in luck. I have enough for the both of us. Are you game? Will you spend the night with me?" Wyld's smile bordered on insane. He couldn't stop.

"I would love to. Now, tell me your first memory."

Wyld gave the question some thought. He let his mind wander. His angel had made a demand. It was one Wyld intended to fulfill. He would spend the entire night talking to Micah, drawing him in, and making him want more. One day soon, Micah would wake up and wonder when Wyld took over his life. At the beginning was the perfect place to start.

THREE

BETWEEN SPENDING the whole night talking to
Wyld on the phone, and knowing he was free for the
next three months, Micah felt lighter than he had in
ages. Since he'd given up before finding the final
stragglers on his meal list yesterday, he'd promised
himself he'd go back out today and try again.
Normally, he would've tried a little harder to find
each person, but he'd been sick of Detroit. Once he'd
finished with his list, who knew. Maybe he'd give
Wyld another call. His cheeks hurt every time he
thought the man's name. He'd listened to Wyld talk
for hours about every little ridiculous thing. Micah
couldn't wait to do it again.

Micah grabbed some cloth delivery bags and
headed for the kitchen. Detroit had done as Micah

asked, and stuffed the meal boxes in the fridge, hoping they would stay good one more day. His steps slowed when low voices floated down the hall. He spotted Detroit first. His dad second. They stood a little too close. Closer than his father and best friend should stand. Micah's heart jumped to his throat. Detroit shuffled even closer. An ache bloomed behind Micah's eyes. His dad ran his knuckles down Detroit's jaw. Everything became clear. The way Detroit always worried about Micah's dad's opinions on things. The way he always showed up early, seeming content to wait for him there until Micah got home. The way he'd stayed Micah's friend through the years, even though they had nothing seemingly in common. It damn sure explained the way Detroit had suddenly started talking down to him a while back, and the distance he'd felt growing between them. Micah couldn't lie to himself. He'd known.

"You're here," Micah said a bit too loud, announcing himself.

Detroit jumped.

His dad turned away.

Detroit's smile was too bright. "Of course, I am. I told you I'd help you track down yesterday's stragglers. You can't carry all those meals on the bus."

The backs of Micah's eyes burned. He couldn't fake another smile. Detroit's betrayal cut too deep. Instead, he put his head down and headed for the fridge. Detroit followed on his heels. Micah fought the urge to snap. To scream he knew the truth. Detroit wasn't his friend. He never had been. All the times that Micah had told people that Detroit hadn't dropped him even though he was him and Micah was Micah choked him now. His heart beat so fast he couldn't think straight. He was always the unwanted one. This was the first time he'd lost to his own father though. That was new.

"Did you tell your dad yet that you left the wedding reception with Wyld West?"

Micah concentrated on breathing evenly as he grabbed the meal boxes from the fridge. He hated confrontation. Nothing good could come of calling Detroit out. "Why would I? I don't expect him to tell me about his private life." He hoped Detroit would take the hint and stop talking.

Naturally, he didn't get his wish. "For fuck's sake, Micah. It's Wyld West. He's bad news. There's only one reason a guy like that would hang out with a guy like you, and we both know he won't get that."

The blow hit its mark. Micah clenched his back teeth and fought back tears. It was the cruelest possible thing Detroit could've said in that moment. All these years, he'd thought Detroit was his friend. The man had used Micah to be near his dad. Then, he had the audacity to throw Micah's biggest secret shame in his face. Only when he thought he could speak without his voice shaking did he respond. "I like him, and some people actually like me for me, Detroit."

"Don't be an idiot."

Rage boiled in Micah's gut. Without warning, he struck, landing a punch in Detroit's gut. He caught the man off guard. That was the only explanation for the way Detroit doubled over. It wasn't the dick punch he'd promised Wyld, but Wyld was right. It was time for him to stop letting people talk down to him.

Detroit held the edge of the counter and sucked air. "What the fuck?"

"Don't you ever call me an idiot again," Micah said, surprising even himself with the growl in his voice. "I will never apologize for caring about people, and I'll be friends with whoever the fuck I want. If you can't accept that, then you can get the hell out and stay out."

Loud clapping came from the opposite side of the room, sending Micah spinning in its direction.

His dad's large frame filled the doorway. "You've had that coming for a while now, Detroit."

Normally, his dad's praise would warm Micah's skin. In this case, he was too damn mad. Even hitting Detroit hadn't helped. He crammed the food trays into bags with more force than necessary.

Detroit massaged the spot where he'd been hit. "Come on, babe," he said quietly, trying to help. "You can't do all this alone."

Micah slapped his hands away. "I've got this. You're free to stay here. We both know that's the real reason you come around anyhow." Without looking back, Micah headed for the door.

His dad tried cutting him off. "Micah."

As his gaze collided with his dad's, Micah couldn't hide the hurt and anger any longer. "Please move." The way his voice shook added to Micah's anger. He hated being weak on top of being unwanted.

The guilt in his father's eyes said it all. "Be careful."

Micah put his head down and barreled outside. He was tired of being the idiot everyone accused him of being. Today was the last day. He couldn't control what people thought of him, but he'd be damned if he'd go on pretending he was blind to the way they treated him.

Wɪ̠ᴅ ꜱᴛᴜᴍʙʟᴇᴅ ꜰʀᴏᴍ ᴛʜᴇ ʙᴀʀ. Hɪꜱ ᴍᴏᴏᴅ darkened by the second. Not the alcohol or the pills made a damn bit of difference any longer. A red-haired guy had followed him to the door, offering him a night most people would die for. All Wyld felt was slightly apathetic. No matter how far he went or eccentric he dressed, no one saw him. Not really. He was money and position. Wyld didn't care. It didn't matter if no one wanted him for him because he didn't care about any of them either. Still, it did get tiresome.

The world blurred and spun. His hand shot out to steady himself against the roof of his car. A cop car passed. Wyld dug out his phone. There was no way he could drive. He squinted at the face of the device. He'd missed two calls from Micah. Wyld's mood lifted. There was one person who saw him. One person who Wyld never got tired of being around.

He clicked on Micah's name and pressed the phone to his ear. It rang twice before his angel's voice caressed his ear.

"Hello?"

"Hello, beautiful angel. What are you wearing right now?"

"Clothes."

Wyld's smile fell. His angel didn't sound happy to hear from him. "Okay," Wyld said, dragging out the word. "Listen, babe. If you're not busy, I could use some help."

Micah's tone changed in an instant. "What's wrong?"

He hated worrying Micah. Wyld could call for a car, but he wanted to see his angel. "My head is spinning, and I can't drive."

"Give me the address." Micah hadn't sounded happy, but he also hadn't hesitated.

"The parking lot of Gentleman Jake's on East Street."

"Stay upright for ten more minutes and I'll be there."

Wyld couldn't stop smiling. "Thank you, Angel." After Wyld hung up, the darkness settled in again. What if Micah didn't show? Even worse, what if he got tired of cleaning up after Wyld—babysitting him? He was hard work. If Micah showed up, Wyld would make it worth his while. The ground swayed again, trying to buck him off his feet. When he sobered up, he'd do better. Everything went black for a moment. Wyld leaned heavily on the side of his car. Something warm touched his face. Wyld's eyes shot open. Micah stood, leaning into him and holding him up. A cab pulled away.

"Where are your keys?"

Wyld blinked, trying to think. "Front left pocket."

Micah didn't hesitate to bury his hand in Wyld's pocket.

"Fuck, Angel. It's a good thing there're way too many fun things racing through my veins to get hard."

Micah's gaze met his and quickly skirted away. "You don't have to make excuses."

Wyld stared at Micah's profile, wishing he had his wits so he could figure out what that was supposed to mean.

"Lean on me," Micah said, urging Wyld to cling to him as he walked him to the passenger side.

Without an ounce of shame, Wyld stole a few extra feels of Micah's delectable body as he allowed the man to lower him into the car. Micah didn't balk. Wyld didn't bother hiding his smirk as Micah circled the car and climbed behind the wheel.

Wyld waited until Micah pulled from the lot

before speaking again. "Thank you for coming for me, Angel."

Micah never looked away from the road. "I've got nothing else."

Wyld mused over the claim. His eyelids grew heavy. Micah hadn't said he had nothing else going on. Just that he had nothing else. The two weren't the same. Once Wyld had some sleep, he'd fix that.

THE CAR FELT EMPTY WITHOUT WYLD'S overbearing personality. Micah fucking hated that Wyld always did this to himself. He was so much more of everything when he was sober. Maybe that was the point. Whatever reason Wyld had for diminishing himself, Micah wished he'd stop. Wyld had been right when he'd called Micah a nurturer. He wanted to help Wyld, but he didn't know how.

At Wyld's house, Micah got Wyld lucid enough to turn off the alarm and walk to the bedroom. Micah stood to the side, watching as Wyld drunkenly stripped. He might've been wrong for not looking away as each new inch of skin bared. Micah told himself he was only ensuring Wyld didn't pass out and kill himself. The truth was, he couldn't look away. Wyld was beautiful. His right thigh and hip were covered in a tattoo of a panther. The rest of his body was untouched perfection. It made the tattoo twice as sexy. He couldn't believe Wyld was so blind. The man spent tons of time with Micah. Yet, he hadn't noticed the way Micah watched his every move, or maybe he had. That thought pissed Micah off and made his chest hurt. That meant Wyld was like everyone else. That meant he was taking advantage of Micah's kindness.

A growl rose in Micah's throat when Wyld stumbled while pulling the covers down the bed. Micah crossed the room and helped Wyld settle beneath the blankets. He smoothed the man's loose curls behind his ears before tracing the line of Wyld's cheek. It ate at his gut, knowing Wyld was killing himself.

"Why are you the way you are?" The question was out there before Micah thought better of it.

Wyld kept his eyes closed. He took a long, exaggerated breath. "Why are *you* the way you are?"

Micah blinked, feeling the blow to his chest. "Okay. I'll leave you alone."

Wyld's hand shot out, snagging Micah's arm before he could get away. His thumb brushed

Micah's skin. Their gazes collided. Wyld held his stare. "There's nothing wrong with you."

That wasn't true. Not in the least. The backs of Micah's eyes burned. "Yes, there is, because people like you think it's okay to call me in the middle night, and I'm stupid enough to come. I'll be here next time too, even though you don't care about me. Not really. Just like Detroit, even though I'm always there for him too. That's how it's always been and how it'll always be until all of you have used me up and I fade away."

Wyld's thumb brushed Micah's arm again, as if he tried soothing him. "Tell me."

Micah's throat swelled. His eyes burned with unshed tears. He swallowed. "He was never my friend." Micah couldn't even say his name. "I don't want to go home."

"Stay here, then," Wyld said, going back to looking ready to pass out. "God knows I've got the room."

Longing slammed into Micah's chest. Wyld offered him a reprieve. Pride wouldn't let him take it. He took a deep breath. "No. I won't be a coward."

Wyld released him and rolled onto his side, facing Micah. "I don't see why not. It works brilliantly for me." Each word came out slurred as if Wyld barely stayed conscious.

A loud sigh escaped Micah. "Scoot over."

Wyld did as told, but not without question. "Why?"

Micah slid under the covers beside Wyld. "Because maybe you're a spoiled ass who doesn't care about anyone except himself, but I care about you. I don't want you to die in the middle of the night from alcohol poisoning."

Wyld tossed a heavy arm across him and tucked Micah against his chest. Micah wanted to protest but the words wouldn't come. "You're wrong," Wyld said, sounding already half asleep. "I care about you."

Micah rubbed the arm draped over his body. "I know you do," Micah whispered the admission in case Wyld had fallen asleep. "I'm just angry tonight."

Wyld's body jerked, as if he'd dozed off and startled himself awake. "Micah."

"Yeah?" He couldn't stop whispering.

"Detroit doesn't deserve you. I know I don't either," he over-pronounced each word, making Micah wonder if he'd remember any of this. "But he's especially stupid. I'd do anything for you."

Micah's eyes wouldn't stop stinging. He didn't know how someone so hated by everyone could make him feel so much. Micah rolled. While using his hands to pillow his cheek, Micah stared at Wyld in the dark. The moonlight filtering through the blinds fell across Wyld's eyes, revealing he stared back. Longing welled inside him. Fear choked him. Micah's pulse pounded in his ears. He inched closer. His skin itched with neglect. No one ever hugged him or kissed him. Everyone wanted sex, but they weren't willing to wait for him to be ready. His heart needed someone's love.

Micah broke. His lips touched Wyld's before he knew it would happen. He backed away every bit as quickly. "I'm sorry. I—"

Wyld's mouth covered his, cutting off his apology. It was a soft kiss. Lips barely parted. Wyld held Micah's bottom lip between his. Micah's heart skipped so many beats, he felt light headed. There was a stirring inside him. Wyld's palm slid down Micah's side. Micah almost jumped away. He forced himself to stay still.

When Wyld pulled away, Micah fought the urge to beg him not to stop. "Don't ever apologize for kissing me." He tugged Micah closer, giving Micah the freedom to bury his face against Wyld's chest.

"You'll stay here until you're ready to go home. If you're never ready to go home, that's fine with me."

Micah stroked Wyld's chest. He felt so warm and real—like he could take away the loneliness. "Okay." Perhaps he was running away from his problems, or maybe he was running toward Wyld. He saw a side of Wyld no one else saw. The man was fascinating and exciting. He was also lonely and miserable. Just like Micah. He couldn't shake the feeling they'd been destined to meet. Plus, Micah was tired of lies. Wyld was a lot of things, but he didn't care enough about anyone or anything to bother lying. He was exactly what Micah needed.

"Wyld?"

"Yeah?"

"I'm sorry I called you a spoiled ass."

Wyld stroked his back. "You're always honest. There's nothing wrong with that. I'm sorry I missed your calls earlier and made you feel like I only called you back when I needed something."

No one would ever understand how amazing it felt for Micah to finally deal with someone who didn't play games or pretend he didn't understand what he'd done wrong. "It's okay. I'm overly sensitive tonight. Otherwise, I know you have a million other people you could've called. You chose me because we're friends."

The silence dragged on long enough Micah thought Wyld had fallen asleep.

"Angel."

Micah smiled against Wyld's chest. "Yeah?"

"We're more than friends."

Without thought, Micah's hold tightened on Wyld. His lips brushed the man's chest, but words were lost to him. Hope was a hard thing to squelch. Micah wasn't sure he wanted to keep fighting. Fuck the bad shit Detroit kept saying about Wyld. Micah couldn't help the way he felt, and Wyld was winning him a little more every day.

MICAH LOOKED ABSOLUTELY GORGEOUS SLEEPING in Wyld's bed. His thick curls were a mess. A smile pulled at the corners of Wyld's mouth. His fingers itched to run through the strands. Wyld's head felt like it was stuffed with cotton. His mouth felt like it had licked all the cotton first. The backs of his eyes itched. He needed water. Micah would need clothes and whatnot when he woke. That was the first step in keeping Micah from backing out of his decision to stay.

Fucking, Detroit. Wyld had been too messed up to find out what that ass had done to upset Micah, but Wyld hated the pain he'd seen in Micah's eyes last night. Wyld needed to do more than give Micah a place to stay. Someone like Detroit wouldn't stop trying to come back in Micah's life. Micah was too nice to stay mad too long.

Wyld rolled from the bed. It was time he stopped waiting for Micah to make every move. Maybe Wyld didn't have much to offer in any form other than monetary, but Wyld had enough money it shouldn't matter. He strode through the house looking for Cortland. Wyld found him making himself a sandwich in the kitchen.

"You're nude," Cortland said in way of greeting.

"It's my house."

Cortland's face didn't as much as twitch. "I was merely pointing out the obvious. It wouldn't be the first time you simply forgot to dress."

Wyld shrugged. "I didn't want to risk waking Micah by looking for clothes."

Cortland tossed an apron Wyld's way.

Wyld easily caught it and wrapped it around his

waist. "Have you done any work today or am I paying you to eat?"

"I earned my money the second I had to look at your dick in the same room as my lunch."

"Touché. Still," Wyld said, getting down to business. "I need you to earn your keep today. You know all those East Coast properties I've been avoiding? I need you to schedule visits for the next three months. Spread them out, so I have time to thoroughly inspect each one. Oh, and Micah will be going with me, so double everything."

Cortland's eyebrows rose. He bit into his sandwich.

The man had been working for him too long. Wyld understood his silent dig for more. "Fucking Detroit Amherst. I don't know what he did to Micah. Well, I have an idea, but still, the fucking fucker. I have to get Micah away from here before he flashes Micah a please fuck me smile and charms his way right back into Micah's life. Damn, I hate that fucker."

Cortland wiped his mouth with a napkin. "I believe we've established he's a fucker."

"Just so," Wyld said, trying to calm down.

"I don't believe I've seen you this up in arms about anything in a long time."

Wyld shrugged. "It's Micah, you know?"

The way Cortland nodded said Wyld had shown his hand. "Yes, I do believe I know. Travel up and down the East Coast, as far away from the fucker as possible, for two, coming up."

Cortland headed for the door, sandwich in hand, and another thought hit Wyld.

"Oh, and Cort, Micah will need clean clothes and whatnot when he wakes up. I can't risk letting him out of sight."

"Of course," Cortland said with a dip of his chin, before leaving Wyld alone.

Wyld had to make this work. Otherwise, it was only a matter of time before Detroit edged him out of Micah's life. After all, he really didn't have anything to offer.

THERE WAS A PILE OF CLOTHES AND AN unopened toothbrush on a chair beside the bed. It was the first thing Micah's gaze landed on when he opened his eyes. There was also a note. With a smile, Micah reached for it.

There are a ton of toiletries in the bathroom. Enjoy your shower. Then, join me for breakfast. — W.

P.S. You're the sexiest sleeper I've ever seen.

P.P.S. It was hard to let you sleep.

P.P.P.S. I already miss your face.

Micah glanced around the huge bedroom. There were four doors to choose from other than the door leading to the hall. He assumed one was the bathroom. As much as he hated to snoop, not only did he need to pee, it seemed he'd be staying here a while. Micah rolled from the bed and scooped up the clothes. They still had the tags on them, making Micah wonder if Wyld had already been out shopping or if they were from a pile of his unworn collection. They were similar in size. Micah could probably wear Wyld's clothes. With a shrug, Micah started opening doors. The first two were closets as big as a normal master bedroom. Thankfully, the third was the bathroom. It was ridiculously opulent. Mirrors covered the walls, each one surrounded by light that seemed to come from around the edges. There was a bathtub big enough for three in the middle of the room, and an open shower that took up one end of the room. It looked complicated. Micah saved that for last. By the time he stepped inside, he was ready for anything. He pushed buttons and turned knobs until hot water hit him from several directions. Micah made it quick, because he hated not knowing how to use something as simple as a shower, and he couldn't wait to see Wyld.

He shamelessly used Wyld's products, trying several things, before dressing. He left his hair dripping as he headed for the kitchen. Even though he'd been there before, he'd never been on a full tour. In truth, Wyld's house was a bit intimidating. It was massive, and everything looked like it cost more than his college tuition. There was also a lot of Wyld's eccentric personality thrown in. That's why Micah loved the place. There were collectors' items from punk rock bands and autographed platinum albums. As much as Micah wanted to move slow and look at everything, he wanted to see Wyld even more. He found him in the kitchen, standing at the island, wearing a "Kiss the Cook" apron and no shirt. Wyld was chopping fruit. Lots of fruit.

He looked up as Micah cleared the doorway. "Good morning, Angel. I hope you like fruit."

Micah stopped at the opposite side of the island and eyed the massive pile. "Good morning. Are you feeding an army?"

Wyld flashed him a sexy smile. "Nah, I've been thinking. Since you're staying here now, you're on holiday from school, and I have business on the East Coast, you should go with. Three full months of seeing the most gorgeous places while stuck with me. Fun times."

Something about being with Wyld flipped Micah's happiness switch. "That doesn't explain this craziness," he said, motioning toward the fruit again.

"Oh, this. Well, I think I must've given my assistant a crazy list while I was high because there's so much fruit here, and we're leaving tomorrow. I figured we'd gorge ourselves. Otherwise, all this will go bad and I hate that."

"You're amazing, but I can't leave. Did you forget, I deliver meals to the homeless each week? The mission will be short a person if I disappeared."

Wyld nodded. His understanding expression never wavered. "Let me ask you this, is it more important to you the homeless get their meals or that you be the one delivering them?"

"That the homeless get their meals, of course."

"Then Cortland can do it for you until we get back," Wyld said, as if the matter was settled.

"Who is Cortland?"

"Cortland!" Wyld bellowed, making Micah jump.

Immediately, a dark haired and super pale man stepped into the kitchen. His smooth features were free of all emotion. He was dressed in expensive looking black pants and a long sleeve black shirt. The man looked perfectly pressed. "Yes, sir?"

Wyld motioned toward him. "This is Cortland. He's my personal assistant. Give him a detailed list of your scheduled stops and he'll make sure everything is taken care of while we're gone."

Micah couldn't stop looking between the two men. "You have a personal assistant?"

"Of course," Wyld said as if he should've been understood.

"Does he live here?" Micah had to know, because he'd never seen the guy, yet he'd appeared in an instant at Wyld's call.

"Yes. How close could he do what I need when I need it done?"

Micah rubbed the spot between his eyes, trying to keep up. "You mean you have a personal assistant who lives in your home, but you called me to pick you up last night."

Wyld eyed him as if trying to figure out Micah's tone. "I wanted to see you."

Micah's stupid heart melted.

A line appeared between Wyld's eyebrows. "Which reminds me, why did you show up in a cab?"

"I don't have a car," Micah said, pointing out what he thought Wyld already knew.

"What do you mean you don't have a car? You took me to the hospital that one day."

"No." Micah dragged out the word. "Technically, Detroit took you to the hospital. I just rode with you. I'm a broke nineteen-year-old college student, Wyld. If it wasn't for my dad, I wouldn't eat most days. There's no way I could buy a car."

Wyld seemed more confused by the second. "How do you usually get around and how did you pay for a cab?"

Micah fought back a smile. "Damn, I see you've never been broke a day in your life. Normally, I take the bus, and I scraped together some change."

"That's it," Wyld said, setting aside his knife. "You're taking one of my cars. I can't have you scraping change together to pick me up or riding the bus." Wyld fake shivered.

Micah lost the battle against his laughter. "We've been over this already. You're not giving me a car. I can't afford the insurance."

Wyld was already back to chopping fruit as if the topic was closed. "Don't worry about the insurance. I've got it."

A frustrated sounding growl escaped Micah. "Normal people don't give people cars, Wyld."

"I'm not normal. Now, give Cortland

instructions for the meal delivery, so he can get back to doing whatever he does all day."

Micah eyed Cortland. Chagrin had him venting. "Can this guy deliver meals with compassion? No offense," he added, tossing a quick glance the assistant's way. "It's more than just delivering food to me. These people deserve to keep their dignity. Quite a few of them have served this country."

Wyld didn't bother looking Cortland's way. "Cortland, do I pay you enough to pretend to have compassion and respect?"

"Of course," Cortland said, sounding bored with their conversation.

"There you go. I plan to show you all the things," Wyld said, sounding bright as he went back to arranging the fruit. It was obvious the matter was settled with Wyld. The man was so damn used to having his way. It was maddening and so freaking hot. They couldn't spend the summer together, going on like this. At least, Micah couldn't. That much time together, pretending he didn't wish Wyld belonged to him, it would kill him.

Something inside Micah snapped. "Would you kiss me?"

Wyld froze at the question, making Micah wonder if he didn't remember their kiss last night.

Wyld's gaze slowly lifted from his chore to meet Micah's. Micah ignored Cortland's presence. He didn't back down. "Would you kiss me, even if there was a possibility it wouldn't go any further?"

Wyld's hungry stare never wavered from Micah as he circled the island. "Cortland, leave."

"Yes, sir."

Micah didn't watch him go. He couldn't look away from Wyld. He'd never seen the man look so intense. Micah's heart sped. He licked his lips. He'd never been more nervous. No one had ever looked at him the way Wyld did. Before he could change his mind, Wyld's body collided with his. Micah was trapped against the edge of the island. "I have all the kisses you'll ever need."

Wyld's mouth came down on his—hard. A moan escaped him before he could stop it from happening. Lust slammed into Micah, nearly knocking his knees out from underneath him. He hadn't expected it. Micah didn't know how to react. Then, Wyld's tongue touched his and nothing mattered except this man's kiss. He'd never been kissed like Wyld kissed him. Slow. Methodical. Perfect.

Another moan slipped out when Wyld's fingers trailed down his body before curling around the waistband of Micah's jeans. A gasp caught in his throat.

Wyld pulled away an inch. Each breath sounded ragged. His eyes were closed. Micah couldn't stop staring at him. He was so damn beautiful. Wyld's eyes opened. Micah had never seen so much heat focused his way.

"I don't expect a damn thing, Angel. But if you ever decide you want me, I'm here, waiting for you."

Micah never stopped being blown away by Wyld. "I'll go with you."

Wyld's triumphant smile made Micah realize Wyld hadn't been as confident as he appeared to be that Micah would go. He pressed another quick kiss to Micah's lips. "Yes." He started to pull away.

Micah snagged his apron and held on. "Also, I want to be with you, but I'm not sure I'm ready for you."

Heat flashed in Wyld's eyes. He leaned in. "I'm not going anywhere. We'll move at any pace you want," he said as the final inch disappeared between them. Wyld's lips brushed his in the lightest kiss. Micah's hands found Wyld's hips, tugging him closer. The move made him realize Wyld was nude beneath the apron.

He leaned away and eyed Wyld's body. "Are you seriously only wearing an apron and nothing else?"

Wyld's smile was unrepentant. "Maybe. Look at it this way, you can bend me over right now and have your way with me."

Micah rolled his eyes and swatted Wyld away. "You're not right. If you're with me, you can't be showing your ass to everyone like that."

With a wink, Wyld circled the island again. "There's no one here but us."

"And Cortland," Micah reminded him as he blatantly watched Wyld's ass as he walked away.

Wyld popped a slice of banana in his mouth. "He doesn't count. First off, he's known me way too long to ever be stupid enough to want me. Secondly, I pay him to see nothing. Now, eat," he said, pointing at the counter. "When you're finished, we'll bag up what's left and take it to your mission place so it doesn't go to waste."

Micah bit his lip, trying to fight back the happiness that threatened to burst from him. Wyld was amazing. He hid it from everyone else, but Micah saw the real him.

"I like you better when you're sober," Micah said, because he felt like someone should.

Wyld curled his nose and ate an orange slice.

"You're the only one." Wyld focused his heated gaze on Micah, forcing Micah to take a deep breath to keep his racing heart under control. "Luckily, you're also the only one whose opinion matters."

Micah wasn't sure what that meant, but he wouldn't nag. Wyld was who he was, and Micah was falling for him—vice and all.

"When do you turn twenty?"

The question caught Micah off guard. "Next Tuesday, why?"

A huge grin split Wyld's face. "Brilliant. First, we'll hit the mission and then it's shopping trip time. I'm buying you everything for your birthday."

Micah's cheeks heated. He wasn't used to getting attention. "Please don't. Usually, my dad just takes me dinner."

"That's your dad. I'm not your dad."

Micah couldn't have stopped the question from leaving his lips even if he'd literally bitten off his tongue. "What are you?"

Wyld's expression turned serious, showing his genuine side. The side Micah couldn't resist. "I'm pretty sure I'm yours. Such as I am. If you'll have me, that is."

A lump formed in his throat. Micah recognized his response would change them. He could crack a joke, and he knew Wyld would go on as his friend. Or he could reach for what he wanted and risk it all on a man no one else believed was worthwhile. Micah felt himself nod. "You're mine."

Wyld's smile was back. "You can't take it back. Now you have to let me spoil you."

A groan rose in Micah's throat, but he didn't mean it. He couldn't wait to see what Wyld did next. They were both obviously out of their element, finding their way together. The future had never looked brighter.

THE LIST OF THINGS WYLD BOUGHT MICAH FOR their summer-long adventure was massive. Micah kept thinking he should balk. There was something about Wyld. He made Micah behave in ways he never expected and accept things in a way he never thought he could. If anyone else had demanded he needed a whole new wardrobe, Micah would've put his foot down. By the time Wyld had finished a lecture with fifteen side trips about how they'd be visiting places with strict dress codes, Micah would've agreed to anything to make him stop talking. Sexy accent aside, Micah recognized Wyld could wear a man down when he wanted.

Horror tried setting in as Micah stood in the center of Wyld's bedroom surrounded by bags and new luggage. He didn't know where to start. Wyld's arms encircled his waist, drawing Micah back against his chest. Micah's eyes fell closed as Wyld's lips touched his neck.

"You should let Cortland pack everything for you. I promise, he's so ready to be free of me for three months, he'd whistle while ensuring you have everything you need."

"I don't mind doing it. It's more that I'm feeling a bit overwhelmed."

"You should definitely say fuck it then and let me take care of you."

Micah couldn't stop his tired chuckle. "I think you've done enough for the day."

"Nope," Wyld said, dragging him toward the bed. "I have two areas of expertise. Driving people insane and putting them to sleep. Come on. Climb in," he urged, lifting the covers.

"Are you sure you don't want me to sleep in a guest room?"

Wyld smirked. "Get in my bed, Angel."

Damn. Micah didn't know how to resist the heat in Wyld's voice. He climbed beneath the covers. After turning off all the lights, doing very little to darken the room since the sun was still up, Wyld climbed in beside him. Once he was settled, Wyld tugged Micah into his arms. Micah's head rested on Wyld's chest. His hand flattened against the man's stomach. Micah's eyes fell closed as the sound of Wyld's heartbeat caressed his ear. He breathed in Wyld's scent. He smelled like fresh air. The thought made Micah smile. Wyld smelled exactly like hope for a new day.

"I can feel your smile." Wyld's voice sounded deeper with Micah's ear pressed to his chest.

"It's been a good day." Micah stroked Wyld's stomach as he made the claim.

Wyld covered his hand, holding it still. "You're too much of a temptation."

Micah's smile grew. "Sorry." He tried settling back down.

"Would it be okay if I kissed you again?"

Instead of answering, Micah lifted up and kissed Wyld. Unlike everyone Micah had kissed in the past, Wyld didn't grope him or try to go farther. He buried his fingers in Micah's hair and held on. Wyld kissed him like he felt something. Deep emotions settled in his chest. On their sides with nothing touching but their lips, time passed without them. They tasted each other, savoring their afternoon alone. Micah never felt pressured for more. It wasn't sexual. Life was reminding Micah he was blessed.

Wyld found Micah's hand. Micah smiled against Wyld's lips as Wyld toyed with each of his fingers. There was so much happiness inside Micah, he didn't know where to go with it. Tomorrow, they'd be thousands of miles away, still enjoying each other. Micah had never felt so full.

FOUR

AT THE ENTRANCE to the Den of Payne, Detroit scanned his membership card to unlock the door and let himself inside. He didn't bother searching the playrooms for Payne. As long as Detroit had been coming here, Payne had only played with the highest paying customers and only then if he was in the mood. Detroit headed for the man's office. The door was closed. He knocked. No response came. Detroit knew Payne was there. He swore he could feel the man's powerful presence on the other side of the door. No doubt Payne had seen him coming on the security cameras. Detroit knocked again. No answer.

He pressed his forehead to the door and squeezed his eyes shut. If only Payne would talk to him. Detroit could make this right. "I know you're in there," Detroit said, uncaring of his pride. "Please talk to me." Nothing. Detroit would sink to any level. "I have news about Micah." The door swung open so fast Detroit almost fell over.

Payne yanked him inside and slammed the door closed behind him. He hovered over Detroit. Those damn mismatched eyes that haunted Detroit's dreams narrowed with rage. "Don't ever speak my son's name inside this club," Payne hissed as he shoved Detroit against the closed door.

Detroit had never seen Payne like this. He knew he was protective of Micah. That's why Detroit tried so hard to keep him safe. Micah was so damn trusting and innocent. There was no saving Micah from himself. His gaze skirted away from Payne's intensity. "I'm sorry."

Payne cupped his jaw, and squeezed, forcing Detroit to hold his stare. Detroit's heart sped. His mouth went dry. He couldn't stay away. There was no one else like Payne. "It's okay. Did you find him?"

"No. I followed his usual route today, thinking there was no way he'd skip out on his duties with the mission. There was this haughty guy named Cortland filling in for him. I tried asking if he knew what happened to Micah. He asked if I was Detroit. When I said I was, he said I could go fuck myself and hell would freeze before he told me shit."

Payne shoved Detroit aside, going for the doorknob. "I guarantee he'll fucking talk to me."

Detroit blocked the door. "Don't bother. I found another way to get the info you need."

Payne's impatience was etched in every line of his body. Detroit expected him to snap at any moment. "Where the fuck is my son, Detroit?"

Detroit flattened his palms against Payne's chest, trying to soothe him. "I went to the mission and talked to Father Brian. He said Cortland was sent by his boss to fill in for Micah while Micah went on a tour of the country."

Payne's face screwed up in confusion. "What the fuck? He doesn't have the money to tour the country."

"There's more." God only knew how badly Detroit wished there wasn't more. "Father Brian said Micah won't return to his duties until the fall."

Payne's features blanked. A cold chill ran down Detroit's spine. There wasn't a doubt in Detroit's mind Payne had just withdrawn every bit of his affection for him. Payne traced Detroit's jaw with his fingertips. His gaze followed the motion. Detroit swallowed. There was ice in Payne's stare. "You're so beautiful." Detroit swallowed. Payne's words sounded like an accusation rather than a compliment. "I'm sure you would love it if I bent you over this desk right now and lived up to my name." Payne shoved. The back of Detroit's head hit the closed door. Payne held him there. He dipped his head. At the last second, Payne changed directions and pressed his lips to Detroit's throat. His wide frame felt intimidating rather than safe. Detroit fought the urge to touch him. Run his fingers through the blond curls he loved. "Don't let me ever see you around here again. Because of you, my son hates me." Payne released him and turned away.

Detroit couldn't move. "I'm sorry, Payne. Tell me what I can do." He'd never felt more helpless.

"You've done enough," Payne said, refusing to look at him. "Micah is all I have, and you knew that. Now, he's god knows where, thinking the worst of me, because I couldn't stay away from you. It won't happen again."

It was like dying. For the rest of his life, Detroit knew he'd remember this moment, and never be the same.

By the time they made it to their first destination, Micah was noticeably wiped. Wyld wasn't feeling his best either. He'd gotten out of the habit of traveling and forgotten how exhausting it could be. They fell across the large hotel bed without bothering to check out the entire suite. There was no missing that everything was white. That was a shame. Wyld fully intended to make a mess of it all. He unbuttoned the shirt he'd only worn for Micah's sake, getting comfortable before slinging his arm over his eyes, and settling in. All he needed was a thirty-minute nap. Then, he would be all Micah's.

Micah's phone rang for the fifth time since exiting the plane.

Wyld peeked out from beneath his arm and eyed Micah. "Is that your phone again?"

Micah looked guilty. "Yeah. I'll turn it off."

"Is it Detroit?" Wyld tried to keep the distaste from his voice.

Micah shook his head. "I blocked his number before we left town. It's my dad."

"You should answer it," Wyld said without thought. "He's probably worried."

Micah chewed his bottom lip. "Are you sure?"

"Of course. No matter what, he'll always be your father."

66

Micah's phone stopped ringing and immediately started again. He answered, sounding unsure. "Hello? Hey, Dad."

Wyld rolled onto his side. He toyed with Micah's curls while shamelessly listening to Micah's side of the conversation. "Yeah, I... Okay. No, I..." Micah blew out a breath. It was obvious he wasn't allowed to get a word in. "No."

Wyld was dying to know what was being said.

"I'm not coming home anytime soon. If you'd let me talk, I'll tell you."

Wyld froze with his fingers in Micah's hair. He hung on every word.

"Seriously? Detroit didn't tell you? I expected the two of you shared everything." An ugly sounding snort escaped Micah. Wyld didn't like it. It didn't suit his angel. "My friend, Wyld."

"I'm more than a friend," Wyld reminded him, even though he knew Micah wasn't listening.

"Yes, that Wyld."

"What?" The shout sounded so loudly through the phone, Micah was forced to move the device away from his face.

A chuckle escaped Wyld. "I see my reputation precedes me."

Micah winked and went back to listening to his

lecture. "Do whatever you feel is necessary. I just wanted you to know I'm okay. We'll be back in California before school starts back. Talk to you later." He hung up and quickly turned off the device before tossing it aside.

"That went well," Micah said, flashing Wyld a sweet smile.

Wyld shifted positions and straddled Micah's hips. He cupped Micah's face, stroking and massaging, hoping to take away the strain. "My poor sexy angel. Tell me how to make it better."

Micah's hands ran up Wyld's thighs. "He'll get over it. No one can see how happy you make me and still stand against us."

With that one statement, Micah proved he'd never been truly hated. Everyone hated Wyld. People could and would continue hating him no matter what. "I hope you're right, Angel. It's not my intention to steal you from your family." It really wasn't, but neither could Wyld consider losing Micah when his family stood against them. Wyld had never met a single person who cared about him for anything other than what he could do for them. Micah didn't give a damn about Wyld's money. Wyld was convinced Micah would still want to be near him even if he lived in a cardboard box. That knowledge fucked with his head.

Micah pushed open the two halves of Wyld's shirt before dragging the material down his arms. Lust darkened Micah's eyes as he bared Wyld's torso. "You're so gorgeous. Have I told you that lately?"

"Hmmm," Wyld hummed. "I'm not sure I remember hearing anything like that from you."

"Very sexy," Micah said while wearing his best indulgent smile.

"Are you trying to change the subject because you don't want to tell me what was said, or because you want me to make you feel better? Either way, I'm game."

Micah kept his gaze locked on his fingers as he dragged them down Wyld's stomach. "He told me to come home. I refused. He threatened to toss my things in the street. I told him to do whatever he felt he needed to do."

"That seems a bit extreme."

Micah's expression turned sad. "I'm not sure he knows how to respond to all this, since I've never stood against him before. The thing is, I'm not trying to run away. Not really. It's just..." Micah held his gaze, making Wyld proud of how strong he was. "I told Detroit everything. He was my best friend. Now, I feel like that friendship was a lie. I feel like I exposed all of my heart to someone who only listened because they were waiting for the time they could be with my dad. It's hard to explain. I feel..."

"Used," Wyld supplied.

Micah nodded. His features changed as if an idea struck. He looked panicked. "I hope you don't think I'm using you to get away from them?"

A snort escaped Wyld. "No. We're here because I insisted. I never do anything altruistically, Angel. If you had told me no, I would've found another way to get you here, because I want you here. With that said, it's not my intention to come between your family and you." Wyld didn't like this new guilt thing Micah made him feel.

Something wicked flashed in Micah's eyes. "Mr. West, I think you're turning soft."

"I'm anything but soft," Wyld said, coming down on top of Micah hard, squishing him to the bed. He kissed every place he could reach with Micah half-heartedly trying to push him away. His laughter was everything, melting Wyld's heart. Wyld finally managed to snag Micah's wrists and pin them to the mattress. Micah stopped struggling. His laughter died away and his expression turned heated. Wyld slowly lowered his head. Micah lifted, meeting him halfway. Their lips brushed. Wyld fought to breathe with Micah kissing him. Something about him affected Wyld in a way no one else ever had before. Micah was hard for him. There was no hiding it. Wyld wanted to make him fly. Without thought, he rocked against Micah, purposely grinding against his erection. He heard Micah's breath catch at the back of his throat.

The memory of Micah saying he wasn't ready for him slammed into Wyld. With a groan, Wyld tore his mouth away. He rolled to his side. With one leg slung over Micah's, keeping him pinned in place, Wyld tried thinking of anything other than his raging hard on.

"I know about your dad. What about your mom?" he asked, desperately trying to cling to his sanity. This whole respect and caring thing was murder on his balls. They'd be blue for months.

The flush on Micah's cheeks told one story—he wanted everything Wyld did, but he still let Wyld change the subject. He cleared his throat. "Um. My mom was a missionary."

"Why am I not surprised? I knew all that awesomeness came from somewhere."

Micah blushed. "Stop. You always make me out

to be so selfless. In truth, I don't know what I am." Micah shrugged. His lips twisted, making him look like a guilty child. "I did idolize her though. She did sort of a Doctors Without Borders thing, traveling and helping people. She took me along until I turned thirteen. Then, she decided I should have a shot at a normal life. She left me with my dad. At first, I thought it wouldn't last long, so I'd make the best of it. Two months later, she was murdered when the area she was in was occupied by soldiers." Wyld's throat swelled at the pain in Micah's eyes. In that moment, he would've given anything to bring back Micah's mother. No one was less deserving of pain than his sweet angel. Micah cleared his throat again. "Anyhow, I started going to the local mission, trying to find ways to help. I don't think I have what it takes to be like her, but neither can I pretend I don't see people suffering while I do nothing." The passion was back in Micah's eyes and voice. Wyld was struck anew by how amazing Micah was, and how undeserving the world was of him. Micah blushed again. His gaze skirted away. "Why are you looking at me like that?"

Wyld tried rearranging his features even though he didn't know what expression he wore. "How am I looking at you?"

Micah bit his lip. A fresh wave of hunger slammed into Wyld. Micah cleared his throat. "Like I'll be nude soon."

He couldn't let the opportunity pass without comment. "Do you think you could handle that?"

While staring at the ceiling, Micah scratched the bridge of his nose. "Um, I'm not sure."

He was adorable. Wyld felt out of his element amongst so much innocence, but he wasn't backing down from this chance. Micah hadn't shut him down yet. "What if I promise no penetration? Just more of a getting to know each other session?"

Micah's head turned. Their gazes met. "Okay."

With that one word, Micah sealed his fate. Wyld would ensure Micah never looked back.

———

WYLD ALWAYS LOOKED SLIGHTLY BORED AND over the top cocky. This version of Wyld—aroused and focused—made Micah's skin feel too tight. Nervousness took a backseat to desire. Wyld tossed his shirt to the floor. Micah shed his too because he needed something to do with his hands. Before he settled onto his back once more, Wyld kissed his stomach, opened mouthed and licking. Micah closed his eyes and held Wyld's head between his hands. He savored each sensation. Wyld cared about him. It was in his every glance and touch. Micah felt like he'd known the man his whole life. He'd never felt so close to anyone.

The button of his jeans loosened. Wyld slid Micah's zipper down. "If I make you uncomfortable in any way, just tell me to stop."

Micah didn't think his tongue would work to say anything at all. His entire being stayed locked on the way Wyld stared at his body as he bared each new inch. No one had ever singed his skin with just a look the way Wyld did. Micah felt the same when he looked at Wyld. He hadn't been flattering the man earlier. There was no one more beautiful than Wyld in Micah's eyes.

Once they were nude, Micah tried keeping his mind blank. He didn't want to panic or overthink things. That's where things had always gone south in the past. Wyld wasn't pressuring him. They were already farther along than he'd ever gotten with anyone else. Micah didn't want to stop. He couldn't fight the small burst of fear that crept in when Wyld covered his body with his. What if he failed at this? Would Wyld decide he wanted to be just friends? Micah didn't think he could take the rejection.

As if sensing his internal freak out, Wyld kissed him. It was sweet and perfect. Gentle. "I promise no penetration," Wyld reminded him against his lips. "No pressure. I only want your time."

Micah tried making his brain work. Why did he care again? Wyld's bare skin went flush against his. A gasp escaped Micah at the contact. They felt like two halves becoming a whole. Wyld braced his palms against the bed and pivoted his hips. The move had their erections massaging each other. Micah lifted his hips, mimicking Wyld's every move. The friction increased between them.

Wyld touched his lips to the shell of Micah's ear. His voice was low and sultry, enticing Micah to keep pace with him. "That's it, Angel. My cock loves touching yours. They belong together. *Mhmmm*, I can feel your pre-cum coating my dick. So sexy. We're moving slow right now," Wyld said, as he gripped Micah's hip with one hand and controlled their pace. "One day soon, I'll lick my way down your gorgeous body and suck your dick until you scream my name. Can you feel it already? My tongue lapping at your crown? Damn, Angel. You feel perfect against me." The sound of Wyld's breath catching against his ear almost sent Micah flying. He'd never pictured making love like this. It had always been embarrassing and uncomfortable in his head. Wyld always turned everything into something beautiful.

He pushed Micah's thighs farther apart and changed angles. The move had Wyld's erection sliding against his with the perfect pressure to make him insane. The pleasure was a slow build. Micah fought the urge to shove his hand between them and move things along. Every ragged breath Wyld took sounded loud against his ear as Wyld sucked on his earlobe. Sounds came from the back of Micah's throat. He couldn't swallow them down.

"Talk to me, Angel. Do you want to feel me riding your dick? Hot, tight, and squeezing you? Or do you need to feel me pushing my way inside? Stretching you and massaging that secret place? Tell me."

Wyld sounded so turned on that Micah couldn't resist him. All his sexy talk and the way his body felt against Micah's, it was stealing away his fears. He pictured all the pleasures Wyld described.

"Both."

At his answer, a deep moan came from Wyld as if he barely held onto his sanity. The sound was empowering and sexy. His motions quickened. Pressure built, itching at the base of his spine. He needed more. Micah fought the urge to flip Wyld over and take what he wanted. At the same time, he wanted to beg Wyld to fill the aching emptiness inside him. He was half insane with need. Wyld ground down on him while moving faster and faster until the pressure threatened his mind. A shout escaped him as the first wave of ecstasy overcame him. He writhed against Wyld, wanting all of it. Their mouths clashed, licking and sucking as they fought to be closer. The mess between their bodies had them sliding and sticking together. Still, they didn't stop. Micah wasn't sure which of them was more crazed.

"Damn, Angel. It's like you're meant just for me." Wyld went for another deep kiss, stopping Micah from saying a word. His mind was a mess. He knew they hadn't made love in the traditional sense, but it felt just as special to Micah. Wyld made everything fucked up about Micah seem normal and okay—like he reveled in all the things everyone else had rejected about him. Wyld's kiss turned sweet. He held Micah tight. Micah's eyes stung. He stroked every inch of Wyld he could reach. Even if they were never more than they were right now, Micah felt blessed to have met Wyld.

IT AMAZED WYLD HOW QUICKLY HE BECAME addicted to watching Micah sleep. If he looked angelic while awake, Micah was ten times that while dreaming. Wyld couldn't sleep from staring at him. He was like the wisp of a fantasy Wyld couldn't hold. He lived in constant fear Micah would stop seeing him through rose-colored glasses and would hate him like everyone else. Wyld felt sick to his stomach each time he thought about changing in Micah's eyes. Damned if he knew how to keep him. He'd never tried making anyone else happy.

Micah's eyes fluttered open. A smile stretched his lips when he caught Wyld staring. "What are you doing?"

"Dreaming with my eyes open," Wyld answered without thought. "I didn't mean to wake you."

Micah's gaze moved over Wyld's face. "I think you're easily the most beautiful man I've ever seen. How did I get so lucky?" Micah whispered.

Wyld's throat swelled. There was so much goodness inside Micah. He was like a beacon in an otherwise bleak world. "I'm spoiled."

A bright smile lit Micah's face. "What does that have to do with anything?"

Wyld inched closer and toyed with Micah's curls. "The day we met, I took one look at you and my heart sped. For the first time in years, I felt a spark of life. I wanted to dance, paint, sing, and I'm greedy enough that I refuse to deny myself the joy of being with you. You're the reason I'm spoiled."

The way Micah's eyes softened made Wyld's heart turn over in his chest. "You never stop melting my heart. All I want is to be near you."

Wyld could barely breathe through the emotions pressing in on him. "Stay with me."

"I am," Micah reminded him with a soft chuckle.

"For good," Wyld clarified, feeling desperate. He'd never been scared before now. Every time he looked at Micah, he recognized he had everything to lose. "When all this traveling is done, and real life comes crashing back in, and when everyone tells you I'm a horrible person who cares about nothing, come home to me in spite of it all."

Micah's expression turned sweet, as if he understood Wyld's panic in a way even he didn't. "There's nothing anyone could say about you that would drive me away. You're more likely to get sick of me first."

Fear of rejection kicked up Wyld's nervous tic of

turning everything into a joke. "Do it. Try to drive me away."

Micah's smile turned devilish. Wyld was fascinated. He'd never seen this side of Micah. "You don't think I can wear you out. Is that what I'm hearing?" Micah asked, crawling closer, until he had Wyld on his back. Micah covered Wyld's body with his.

"Pretty sure I didn't say anything about wearing me out, but that's true too. I have a slight hyperactivity issue."

"Let's see if I can help with that," Micah said, dipping his head and capturing Wyld's lips. With Micah, Wyld never assumed anything. He followed Micah's lead. Anything Micah was willing to give, Wyld would be content. That didn't stop him from stroking every place he could reach of Micah's body. Their tongues met and tangled. Wyld adored Micah's kisses. They were as sweet as the man. He was gentle and so fucking hot. He made Wyld want to beg. His entire brain and body were engaged. The building could come down around them and Wyld wouldn't notice.

Micah's lips moved to Wyld's jaw. He nibbled. Wyld's cock ached like he hadn't already had one mind blowing orgasm.

"I want to make love to you."

Wyld froze. He worried he might've only heard what he wanted. A fine sheen of sweat broke out on his skin. That's how much his desire owned him.

"But I don't have a condom or anything," Micah added. A hint of nervousness sounded in the man's voice.

Wyld didn't want Micah to back down. If he let that happen now, Micah might not try again. He teased Micah's lips back to his. Wyld waited until Micah's body relaxed and his breathing deepened before speaking. "I want you inside me. There's a condom in my wallet."

Micah didn't go for the wallet right away. Instead, he spent another minute kissing Wyld. Their lips clung. Wyld had never felt so calm and complete, yet ready to scream his happiness at the same time before. Each time Micah touched him, Wyld saw a greater plan in the works. He was oddly nervous on Micah's behalf. Wyld didn't remember ever being innocent. Micah gave him a second chance at life.

Micah cupped Wyld's face and held him in place. "Wyld," Micah whispered between kisses.

"Angel."

"I'm scared of disappointing you."

Never. There was nothing his angel of miracles could ever do to let him down. "The thought of you touching me has me ready to explode. Will you be disillusioned and leave me when I can't last?"

Micah shifted to his knees and grabbed Wyld's wallet. He handed it over. Showing his inner strength, Micah held Wyld's stare as Wyld dug out the condom. After tearing open the package, Wyld rolled the sheath down Micah's length. The intense and determined way Micah watched his every move had Wyld ready to burst.

"You can still say no," Micah said, sounding ridiculously turned on. The idea nearly snapped Wyld's mind. Micah wasn't aroused by lust in itself as he'd freely admitted once. He needed a deep connection. Knowing that Micah felt something for him, something powerful and to his core, it was Wyld's undoing. He had to drink it in, savor Micah's affection.

"Please, don't stop." Even Wyld heard a desperate note in his voice that he'd never used before. There was no going back for him. Being with Micah was as necessary as breathing.

"I won't," Micah swore as he recaptured Wyld's lips. He urged Wyld's knees higher. Wyld moved at Micah's pace even though lust scratched at his brain and ripped at his skin. A moan escaped when Micah toyed with his asshole. He was so hungry. Life had been so damn dull and meaningless. Everything was new again in Micah's arms. He couldn't control the sounds vibrating in his throat. As if Wyld's audible pleasure drove him, Micah's cock probed his ass. Wyld held his breath. Micah pushed his way inside. His angel gasped as Wyld scrambled to keep his sanity. The delicious pressure and pleasure ruled him.

Micah pressed his forehead to Wyld's chest and buried himself deep. "You're so beautiful," Micah whispered, slaying Wyld. Micah rocked inside him. The sound that came from Micah's throat had pre-cum dripping onto Wyld's stomach. He wanted to stroke his cock, but he was already too close. Not only had Micah restored color to his life, Wyld hadn't been this sober in ages. Every sensation was heightened like he hadn't experienced in years.

Micah moved slow, making love to Wyld. He cupped Wyld's face and held his stare as he pumped inside him. Wyld lost himself. They were united in a way he couldn't explain. They were intensely connected. His balls drew up tight. Pleasure beat at his crown, begging for release. Wyld wasn't sure he blinked. He couldn't look away from Micah. A gasp escaped him. He was so close. Wyld knew he could reach between their bodies and take his pleasure. Instead, he waited, savoring each passing second. Wyld didn't want their moment to end. Micah shifted higher, but his gaze never wavered. The move had Micah hitting something internally at the perfect angle. A whimper escaped Wyld as an orgasm slammed into him. Cum coated their skin.

Micah's lips parted on a breath. The flush on his cheeks deepened. His intensity doubled. Wyld swore the man's expression alone had him ready to explode again.

Micah's eyes fell closed. A muscle jumped in his jaw. He was silent as he came. Wyld was transfixed. It was the hottest orgasm he'd ever witnessed. Micah's eyes opened. He looked almost frighteningly focused as he lowered his head and captured Wyld's lips in a bruising kiss. His weight lowered onto Wyld, uncaring of the cum coating the space between them. Micah's mouth moved to Wyld's ear. Light kisses touched the shell of Wyld's ear, stealing his heart. "I want to stay with you," Micah whispered against his ear, sounding winded. "When we get back to California, if you were serious in your offer, I want to stay."

The backs of Wyld's eyes stung and his throat

swelled. No one had chosen him for him the way Micah had. He couldn't get enough. It was overwhelming. "I meant every word. I want you with me always."

Their lips met on the claim—like sealing a promise. Micah had agreed to be his. Wyld's life was complete.

FIVE

THE MOONLIGHT SHIMMERING across the ocean didn't hold a candle to Micah's beauty. Key Largo was a beautiful place, even in the dark, but Micah was all Wyld saw. They'd been walking along the beach for ten minutes. Wyld wasn't sure how he hadn't tripped. His gaze hadn't once wavered from Micah. Barefoot and wearing nothing but shorts, he looked every bit the angel Wyld always accused him of being. The breeze coming off the ocean kept rippling his curls. Wyld's fingers itched to touch them. This was the third town they'd been in, and Wyld hadn't accomplished a thing business-wise. Micah was a different story. It felt like they were building something together.

Micah stopped. He stared out over the water. "It's beautiful here."

Wyld didn't bother looking away from Micah. "It is."

Micah glanced over. "I bet you've seen some amazing places. Where's the most beautiful place you've ever been?"

"The alley behind the Den of Payne."

A sharp laugh escaped Micah. "What?"

"That's the first place I saw you," Wyld explained.

"I was being serious."

"So am I," Wyld countered. "The first time I saw you in that alley..." Wyld shook his head.

"You were bleeding," Micah reminded him with a smile. His smile fell. "Someone had obviously hit you."

Wyld waved off Micah's concern. "I deserved it. I think. Hell, I don't know. I was pretty messed up that day. There's no sense in boring you with what all I'd done, hoping to feel something, or I don't know. Maybe hoping I wouldn't ever feel anything again." Wyld shifted from foot to foot and stared out at the ocean. The warm breeze across his skin reminded him he was alive and drove him to confess things better left unsaid. "I thought you were a hallucination at first." A sardonic smile pulled at Wyld's lips. He had been more fucked up that day than he cared to admit. "When you have as much material things as I do, you're not allowed to be unhappy, because so many people have real struggles. But everyone feels the way they feel, and I was miserable." Wyld turned his head and held Micah's gaze. "Then you were there. Thank you. I know meeting me has been nothing but grief for you. It's meant everything to me."

"Meeting you hasn't been grief for me. Why would you even think that?"

Wyld shrugged and shook his head. "You're having to keep your phone turned off to stop people from calling to lecture you about me. You shouldn't have to do that. I feel like I'm costing you too much."

"Ugh," Micah growled as he closed the distance between them. He buried his arms inside Wyld's open shirt and wrapped them around Wyld's waist. Micah held his stare as if trying to make Wyld comprehend his seriousness. "Everyone thinks I'm dumb. That didn't start when I met you. It's always been that way. Me being with you, they all think that's just a new edition to the Micah is ridiculously naïve show." Micah's voice turned deep and mocking. "Micah doesn't gush over hot guys, go to strip clubs or party. He must not be right in the head. Micah's always picking through back alleys, looking for the homeless. Someday, he'll turn up dead for being ridiculous." A sad smile touched Micah's lips. The sight made Wyld's throat swell. He held tighter to Micah, letting him say all the things he'd obviously kept bottled inside. "I'm not stupid."

"Bloody right you're not," Wyld said hotly, but Micah kept talking over him.

"And it's not your fault I'm angry with everyone. They just see me being with you as an extension of what they already believed to be true about me. I don't want to feel the way they make me feel any longer. Since I can't change who I am, what other choices do I have?"

"All the choices in the world, Angel, because you have me. I'll always take care of you."

Micah touched his forehead to Wyld's. Wyld couldn't look away from his angel's eyes. "You're the first place I've felt normal," Micah whispered.

The words punched Wyld in the chest. They mimicked how Wyld felt—like Micah was his home. Wyld ran his hands up Micah's back and held on. Eventually, they would go home. When that day came, Wyld was scared shitless Micah wouldn't be able to keep shutting out the voices of the people he loved. Wyld also scared himself a little. If anyone spoke to Micah the way they always did, Wyld feared for their safety. Micah was perfect. He didn't need anyone to change him or school him on real life. The beautiful spark inside Micah deserved to be cherished.

"Fuck normal, baby. You're extraordinary."

Micah's eyes fell closed, as if he savored the words. The sight stole Wyld's breath. There was nothing fake or contrived about Micah. The little things always seemed to mean the most to him—like he'd been starved of affection. Wyld wouldn't stop. He'd never quit trying for this same reaction. It was more powerful than any drug.

Wyld took advantage of Micah's closed eyes and stole a kiss. It was a simple brushing of lips, but Micah's hold tightened. A chant started in Wyld's head and wouldn't relent. *Please love me. I'll give you everything. Please love me.* He couldn't stop. His heart didn't care that his brain didn't believe in love. Micah was the one for him.

SIX

THROUGH TWO MONTHS of being together constantly and countless towns, Micah wanted more. He didn't want to go back to California. Too many times to count, he'd considered begging Wyld to keep moving. Find another city or country for them. But the mission was counting on him. He couldn't abandon Driver most especially. No other volunteers would take the time to hunt the man down each week to ensure his needs were met. He didn't doubt for a second that Detroit hadn't bothered going to the mission at all since he'd been gone. The instant Detroit's name floated through Micah's mind, he shoved it aside. It hurt too much to think about the friend who'd never really been his friend at all. Maybe back when Micah had been fourteen and

Detroit was sixteen and not that different from each other, but now they had nothing. Micah had become a means to an end for Detroit. The knowledge broke Micah more than he could withstand.

"What do you think of this place?" Wyld asked, pulling Micah from his dreary thoughts.

Micah eyed the tree-lined road. There was nothing but forest as far as the eye could see. "It's peaceful."

"Do you think I should buy it?"

Micah glanced around, trying to wrap his mind around the question. "Like, all of it?" He wanted to take Wyld's question seriously. No one else treated him as their equal.

"This area was ravaged by wild fires a few years back," Wyld explained. "It used to be a big vacation spot before then. You know, cabins and stuff for secluded getaways. I'd like to rebuild it."

It hit Micah. Wyld was more than a bad boy with odd tastes. He was an expert in his field. "That sounds like an amazing investment."

Wyld nodded while keeping his eyes on the road. "Most of this land is owned by three business partners. Their families have held onto it for generations. I've tried buying it in the past, digitally, without ever meeting in person. They wouldn't sell.

Meanwhile, more and more local businesses are closing because of lack of tourists. Real people are losing everything and having to move away from the only lives they've ever known." Wyld glanced over, looking more serious than he'd ever seen the man. "I want to rebuild and put a stop to all that."

Damn. Micah loved this man. His brain screeched to a halt. For a moment, Micah stared at Wyld's profile, frozen by his own thoughts. It was true. Micah loved him. He was so amazing. It was blinding. "What'll it take to convince them to sell?" Micah would do anything to feed Wyld's desire to help others.

Wyld flashed him a smile. "That's what we're about to find out. This is the first time they've been willing to meet with me in person. That's a start."

"I'll stay out of your way."

Wyld reached over and linked fingers with Micah. "You're never in the way. I love having you with me. Thank you for agreeing to do this with me. I know some of these meetings have you feeling out of place, but I wouldn't want to be with anyone else."

Micah chewed the inside of his cheek to keep his ridiculous smile in check. Wyld was right. A lot of places they went were out of Micah's comfort zone. As long as he was with Wyld, Micah would deal. Not to mention, it was hard to feel too out of place with someone like Wyld. He rarely put on a shirt. If he did, it was a button down he refused to button. He almost always looked like he'd just rolled out of bed and draped his body in half of the world's most outlandish and high-priced suits. Yet, he was still the sexiest man in the room everywhere he went. All eyes always followed him. Never with disapproval. People wished they were as brave as him. It was in their envious stares. Wyld was the misbehaved arrogant billionaire of everyone's wet dreams, and he belonged to Micah... for now. All those thoughts died as their destination came in to view.

The country club where Wyld's meeting was being held was leagues above any place Micah had ever been. No one batted an eye as they came through the door. Micah couldn't believe people thought he belonged. He expected an intruder alarm would sound at any moment. Being with Wyld was surreal. He went wherever he wanted, doing and wearing whatever he pleased. No matter how crazy he behaved, people loved him. But it was a fake love. Everyone they met were actors on a stage for a play only they cared about. The more time he spent among Wyld's set, the more Micah realized, as eccentric as Wyld was, he was also the only genuine one in the bunch.

Three men sat in comfy looking chairs, holding whiskey and looking like something out of a backwoods cartoon. If they didn't have antlers and one stuffed lion in their homes, Micah would eat his tie. Their tall cowboy hats and shiny boots were as cliché as they came. Yet, Micah didn't believe for one second any of these men had shoveled shit in their lives.

"Mr. Rogers, so nice of you to meet me."

Micah fought the urge to laugh hysterically at the name. Only the fact the man wasn't wearing a sweater saved him. Otherwise, everything else fit. The older man came to his feet and shook Wyld's hand.

"Mr. West."

"It's just Wyld," Wyld said, brushing off the formalities.

"Wyld," Mr. Rogers repeated with a smile. "You can call me Reed." He motioned toward the two men who'd also come to their feet. "This is Immanuel Bush and Jericho Marks."

Wyld nodded both men's way, before motioning toward Micah. "This is Micah."

Micah flashed a shy smile. He nearly sighed in

relief when they each immediately dismissed him.

Reed reclaimed his seat. "We appreciate you agreeing to meet us in person. I have to say, now that I'm looking at you, I'm even more convinced we shouldn't sell to you."

Micah couldn't stop eyeing Wyld's every reaction. Wyld didn't seem the least bit insulted.

Instead, Wyld smoothed the lapels of his overly loud purple jacket that—of course—he was shirtless beneath. "I know it's not my taste in clothes, because I look damn good, if I do say so myself."

Reed's smile turned indulgent. "I'm not talking about your clothes, Mr. West."

Damn. They were back to formalities. Micah didn't feel confident about this acquisition.

"My concerns have more to do with your lifestyle choices."

Micah fought a wince.

"Around here, people aren't accepting of...." He waved his hand around, as if searching for a way to complete his insulting thoughts.

In a flash, before anyone could've guessed at Wyld's next move, Wyld closed the distance between Reed and himself, and straddled the man's hips. Micah felt every head turn their way as if the quick motion stirred up the wind.

Wide eyed and barely blinking, Micah fought to keep a straight face as Wyld settled in.

"Finish that sentence. I dare you," Wyld said, sounding downright scary as he wrapped his arms around Reed's neck. "Then, I can stand up and the whole room will see, your feelings don't match your words." Wyld dropped his gaze to the man's lap, looking scandalized and leaving no doubt what he meant.

"I was going to say you're single and unstable."

That seemed to give Wyld pause. He motioned toward Micah. "Actually, as you can see, I'm only one of those things. I belong to this one, and—really —he takes care of both those points."

The man's gaze swung Micah's way. Micah tried pasting on his most patient smile. "He's awful young."

"Exactly so," Wyld said, sounding proud. "I'll never have to go looking elsewhere."

"I see your point. If you're truly interested in buying, and this one keeps you reined in, I think we can come to terms."

Micah wasn't sure if the guy gave in because Wyld had convinced him or to get Wyld off his lap. Either way, Wyld finally leapt away. "Brilliant. Do you hear that, Angel? We get to brag to Auntie

Zander that we own a few hotels now too. Of course, this is the Bible belt, so we can't have bet fights, but we can own bears."

"We're not owning bears," Micah said automatically. "That's cruel." He pinched the spot between his eyes where a pain bloomed. "Oh my god. What am I even saying? It's like I don't even know myself anymore."

"See," Wyld said, sounding proud. "He's my conscience."

"You should get your man a drink," Reed offered. "I get the feeling he needs one."

Wyld threw an arm over Micah's shoulders. "One lemonade coming up. My angel isn't old enough for a real drink," Wyld said, steering him toward a nearby bar.

Micah concentrated on blinking, hoping he didn't look like a complete psychopath. Being with Wyld was never dull. "You're completely insane," Micah said under his breath the moment they were out of earshot.

Wyld beamed as if Micah had paid him the highest of compliments. "It's one of my finest qualities, if I do say so myself, and if you're being honest, you'll admit that's how I won you."

Maybe it was. In truth, Micah couldn't narrow it

down to one moment or attribute. From the very first moment they met, Wyld had patiently reeled him in like a master. Whatever quality of Wyld's that had ensnared him, Micah knew one thing for certain—it would kill him if Wyld wanted out. Micah possessed an old and loyal soul. One that attached to people for life. He wasn't sure Wyld could say the same. No matter what, Micah planned to hang on until the bitter end.

MICAH HELD HIS OWN THROUGH THE COUNTRY club debacle. Wyld knew in his heart anyone else would've bolted the second Wyld climbed in that dude's lap. A snort escaped him at the thought. He wasn't embarrassed. It took a lot to make him ashamed, but Micah hadn't batted an eyelash. Nothing screamed loyalty like that, and that type of loyalty deserved a reward.

As Wyld let Micah inside their hotel suite, he tried desperately to keep his features blank until Micah spotted his gift. Micah stepped through the door and froze. Wyld eased in behind him and closed the door, still waiting for a reaction.

Micah rubbed the bridge of his nose and stared

at the six-foot stuffed teddy bear. It was obvious he didn't know whether to laugh or cry. "There's a bear in our room."

Wyld bit his lip to keep from crowing with laughter. "Just a small one. I told you we could own bears now."

The way Micah's disbelieving gaze swung his way said so many things. Mostly that he thought Wyld was crazy. He pointed at the bear. "That's a small one?"

While carefully keeping his face blank, Wyld nodded. "They have them twice this size online, but this was the biggest one they could deliver in two hours. I wanted to surprise you."

"Oh, I'm surprised," Micah muttered under his breath. Wyld still heard every word. Micah covered his mouth, but it did nothing to hide his smile. That was in his eyes. He cleared his throat. Wyld couldn't decide if he was fighting back laughter or didn't know what to say. "What are we supposed to do with this guy until we get home? How are we supposed to get him home for that matter?"

Wyld shrugged. He hadn't thought that far ahead. "I'll hire a car to drive him back for us."

Micah was back to rubbing the bridge of his nose. He no longer tried hiding his smile. "I love him." Before Wyld had time to pat himself on the back, Micah kept talking. "But, he had to have cost a fortune."

"I can afford it," Wyld said with a shrug. "Spoiling you is becoming my favorite pastime."

Micah went back to staring at the bear. He shook his head. "You could do so much good with your money if you bought something other than bears. Do you have any idea how you could change the world? Not just with investments, but for your fellow man."

Wyld crossed his arms over his chest, propped his chin up on his palm, and stared at Micah. He was full of passion and optimism. Wyld hated knowing life would eventually drain Micah of all his hunger to make the world better, but it would. "I'm assuming you have enough ideas for us both."

Micah shook his head, obviously exasperated. "Haven't you even considered what you could do for the town you live in? For the people you pass on the street every day? A majority of the homeless population are dealing with mental health issues, which is becoming an epidemic. With the right funding, we could build a community of tiny houses where they could have a place to live and keep their dignity. We could start return to work programs, so they can eventually move on to paid housing and reclaiming their lives."

"We?"

With a careless wave, Micah huffed. "Yes, we. All of us. The world in general."

Wyld straightened. "You've convinced me to help."

"Really?" Micah sounded hopeful and suspicious—as he should. Wyld never did anything without an ulterior motive.

"I have one condition though. You'll have to marry me."

"What?" Micah all but screeched the word. "Why in the heck would you want to marry me? You don't love me."

A sardonic smile pulled at Wyld's lips. "Love is a myth, Angel. I've been around the block so many times, I have holes in my soles and I've never found love."

"Were you looking?" Micah sounded genuinely curious.

"If love existed the way people claim, it wouldn't matter if I was looking. It would've hit me no matter what. To answer your earlier question, I want to marry you because I like you better than anyone else, but I would never give carte blanche over my money to anyone other than a spouse. Not to mention, you marrying me would have the added bonus of enraging Detroit."

Micah's expression turned sad. He shook his head. "How awful that you'd throw yourself away on me just to piss off someone you don't like."

Wyld closed the distance between them, going flush against Micah. He swiped his fingers through Micah's hair. "Being with you isn't throwing myself away. I'd rather be with you than anyone else on the planet. You're the one who should run. I'm one hundred percent positive you can do better than me, but I won't find anyone better than you."

Micah licked his lips, looking nervous. His hands landed on Wyld's hips, as if he unconsciously tried holding him in place.

Wyld smelled victory. He went in for the kill. "Think of how you could change the world with me backing you."

"You don't love me," Micah said again, sounding sad.

"Does love matter in this equation?"

Micah gave a jerky nod. "It does to me."

Wyld couldn't resist running his hands up Micah's chest and linking his fingers behind the man's neck. "You'd better marry me before I get away. Think about it. If I was a better person, how would you answer?"

"Don't talk like that. You're the best person I know."

A slice of pain cut through Wyld. He fought a wince. "That's the saddest thing I've ever heard you say."

"You may not love me, or yourself, but I love you."

Wyld couldn't hide his wince twice. "Damn, I stand corrected."

A determined look entered Micah's eyes. His hold on Wyld's hips tightened. He towed Wyld closer. "Okay. Let's do it." A triumphant shout rose in Wyld's throat, but Micah wasn't finished. "On one condition."

"Just one? You're a terrible negotiator."

"You have to be faithful to me." Micah made his demand while looking entirely too pleased with himself, as if he knew Wyld would never agree to such a thing. Little did he know, he knew nothing at all.

"Done."

An obnoxious sounding snort escaped Micah. "Just like that? After years of debauchery?"

"Yes." Wyld didn't elaborate. He wouldn't

bother explaining that Micah was the first person to turn him on in years. At the rate he drank and swallowed pills, he probably only had a few years left in him. Not to mention, as strange as it was, Wyld truly didn't have eyes for anyone else. He couldn't explain it. Nor did he care to look at things too closely, but Micah needed to marry him.

"Why?"

Damn. "Because you asked it of me." Funny, the answer came without thought.

The sweetest of Micah's smiles made an appearance. "You'll make me sorry, won't you?"

Wyld didn't hesitate. "Most likely, but you could always divorce me and take me for every penny."

Micah touched his forehead to Wyld's. His beautiful gaze looked even more so up close. "I've been sorry for less."

An unexpected tightness squeezed Wyld's chest. The sensation was new. He wondered for a second if he was having a heart attack. Then Micah's lips touched his, and the ache disappeared.

MICAH MIGHT'VE SEEMED CALM ON THE outside. Inside, he was freaking the fuck out. He'd just agreed to get married. Even he didn't know how it happened. One minute, he'd been passionately speaking about the homeless population. The next, he'd said yes. All his inner protests were dying a swift death as Wyld backed him toward the bathroom. He unbuttoned Micah's shirt, showing amazing multi-tasking skills. Micah couldn't think straight with Wyld's lips on his body. It seemed as if one moment they were kissing, and the next, hot water streamed down their nude bodies in the shower while Wyld held him. There was no space between them. They were molded hip to chest. Wyld's face stayed buried against Micah's neck.

Micah felt like he floated on a cloud. With his eyes closed, he savored the sensation of Wyld softly singing against his throat. Wyld's lips brushed his skin with each word. Micah recognized the love song, but nothing penetrated his brain beyond the sensations of his body. He hadn't known it was possible to love someone so much. He felt full.

Whenever he was with Wyld, it was like goosebumps ran across his brain before traveling down the length of his body. And, damn, he wanted him. It was such an odd sensation to go from rarely feeling any sexual attraction to anyone whatsoever to needing Wyld to make him moan. He could watch porn and nothing. He'd never tell a soul, but he'd also watched Detroit masturbate once, in an attempt to trigger some desire in himself. Nothing. His whole life, it was like he was broken. Then, Wyld had burst into his life and kicked down every wall. Now, fuck, he craved Wyld.

As if Wyld read his thoughts, and knew he couldn't wait another second, Wyld stroked his erection. Micah's head fell back against the shower wall. His hips automatically moved, seeking more. He fought the urge to beg. A whimper escaped instead. Micah had years and years of pent up desire ready for Wyld to unleash.

"Oh, sexy. Make that sound again," Wyld pleaded. His lips brushed Micah's chest, before his teeth scraped Micah's nipple. A gasp tore from Micah's lips.

Wyld dropped to his knees.

Micah dropped his chin toward his chest. He stared down the line of his body. Wyld's sexy eyes flipped upward. Their gazes met. Wyld licked Micah root to tip before taking Micah down his throat. Micah's knees almost buckled as his crown scraped the roof of Wyld's mouth before the man's throat tightened around him.

"Oh, god."

Micah bit his lip, trying to keep from making another sound. Wyld hollowed out his cheeks and sucked. Micah slapped a hand against the wall to stay upright.

"Do it again." He couldn't stop. It was like his lips belonged to a stranger. Micah needed Wyld to keep going. Then, Wyld urged his thighs apart. He fisted Micah's cock as his mouth moved lower. Wyld tongued Micah's balls while his fingers found Micah's asshole. Micah's vision darkened around the edges. He'd never experienced anything like Wyld's touch. Wyld massaged the outer ring, teasing. Micah fought the urge to scream.

"Please?"

He didn't have time for horror over the plea. The tip of Wyld's finger slipped inside him. Each breath Micah took sounded like a shot vibrating off the shower walls. Wyld's hot mouth surrounded his dick once more. A second finger joined the first. As Micah's crown hit the back of Wyld's throat, Micah found himself shamelessly riding Wyld's fingers, racing toward the edge of insanity. Wyld's motions quickened. Micah openly fucked his mouth and fingers, fighting for release. He was so close to ecstasy, he could taste it.

"Feels so good." His mouth wouldn't stop

betraying him. He might be embarrassed later. For now, Micah just wanted the orgasm Wyld promised with his skilled mouth.

Wyld's fingers curled inside him, hitting something. Stars popped behind Micah's closed lids. A loud moan tore from his throat. Pleasure slammed into him, forcing the pressure from his shaft. Wyld didn't stop sucking. Micah could feel him swallowing. The sensation was heaven on his cock.

By the time Wyld moved back to his feet, he was supporting Micah's weight. His knees were jelly, and his head was a mess. Euphoria filled him to completion. Micah fought for air. His mind was fuzzy.

"Just give me a minute," Micah gasped. "I'll make sure you're taken care of too."

Wyld's cheeks were flushed, and he was hard, but he looked calm. "We have all night, gorgeous. There's no hurry." He squirted some shampoo in his hand and started washing Micah's hair as if they truly had all the time in the world. Micah did his best to slow his racing heart. They had the rest of their lives together. He would make Wyld fly soon enough.

SEVEN

WYLD SMOOTHED down the lapels of the black suit he'd bought for the occasion. He was nervous and excited all wrapped into one. Micah's hand covered his, stopping his fidgeting.

"Should I wear a shirt? Do you want me to put on a shirt?"

"Are you joking? Never ask me that again. I love you exactly as you are, and I love your gorgeous body. If it was up to me, you'd never cover up."

"Are you ready for this?"

A line appeared between Micah's eyebrows. "Are you? You sound nervous."

"I'm scared out of my wits that you'll change your mind. If I lose you, I don't know what..." Wyld sucked in a breath, trying to calm his racing heart.

A blinding smile overcame Micah's face. "You're adorable. I'm about to walk into this place and happily say my vows loud and clear. You coming?"

Wyld tucked Micah's hand in the crook of his arm and headed inside the tiny white chapel. The place was surrounded by gorgeous trees and pink flowers. It was the perfect setting for marrying the perfect man. His nerves calmed as they reached the front where the reverend stood, waiting to tie Micah to Wyld for life. Other than the man set to marry them, only his wife was there as witness.

Wyld pulled Micah to a stop before they reached the front. "Are you upset your dad and Detroit aren't here? Would you like me to fly them in first?"

A sweet expression settled on Micah's face. Micah stroked his cheek. "This is our day, baby. I want to remember this day as a beautiful moment for us. As much as I wish people were here supporting us, they wouldn't if they were here. Stop worrying that you're stealing something from me. You're not. I'm overjoyed. Are you, or have you changed your mind?"

Wyld adored that Micah always knew exactly what fueled his moods. He did worry he was stealing something from Micah. His mind couldn't be changed. Rather than explaining that to Micah, he rushed Micah to the front with more enthusiasm than necessary. He practically lifted Micah's feet from the floor in the rush.

Laughter filled the tiny chapel.

"I do. I do," Wyld called, making Micah laugh harder.

"Me too," Micah said, making him proud.

The reverend's smile was indulgent. "You should probably wait until I ask."

"Oh, okay," Wyld said, sounding overly chipper even to his ears. "Ask away, my friend. We're very excited to get started."

"Then let's begin."

Wyld faced Micah and repeated every word he was told to repeat. He watched Micah's lips as he did the same. They flashed each other conspiratorial smiles as they exchanged rings, as if they each silently swore to take over the world together. When they sealed their promises with a kiss, Wyld swore he felt an invisible string tie them together. Micah was his for the rest of his days and Wyld couldn't be prouder.

* * *

FROM HIS SPOT ON THE BED, MICAH WATCHED

Wyld as he talked on the hotel room phone. He wore nothing proudly as he should. It was almost funny that even while missing his usual eccentric attire, Wyld still stood out. He was unique on a cellular level. Micah never tired of trying to work out the puzzle that was Wyld West.

"No. I'll come down and get it myself. There's no telling when a staff member could get around to delivering it." Wyld eyed Micah. "And I might be too busy to answer the door."

Micah bit his bottom lip, holding back a sigh. It wasn't about the sex. Since Micah wasn't one to get turned on for the sake of pleasure, with Wyld their connection went deeper. Anytime Wyld touched Micah, it was as if the man stroked his heart rather than his body. Each encounter left him craving the next.

Wyld hung up the phone. His gaze stayed locked on Micah's face as he crawled onto the bed. Micah's breath caught in his throat at Wyld's intensity. Wyld's lips came down on his, barely brushing before retreating. Micah automatically lifted, trying to reclaim Wyld's kiss without thought. Their lips belonged together. It was unnatural to be apart. Wyld gave him what he sought, kissing him deeply before pulling away again.

"There's paperwork at the front desk I have to pick up. I need to look it over before it heads back to the lawyer's office."

Micah nodded. Despite all the time Wyld dedicated to making Micah's every dream come true, Wyld was there on business. He needed to let the man work. They only had a week left until they went home. "Go do what you need to do."

Wyld pressed another hard kiss to Micah's lips. "Don't move from this spot," he demanded as he pulled away. "I'll be back before you have time to miss me." He headed for the door.

Micah called out, stopping him. "Wyld."

"Yes, my angel."

He couldn't hold back his laughter. "Put some clothes on, please?"

Wyld glanced down at himself and sighed. "How tiresome," he bitched as he grabbed a pair of shorts and pulled them on. He spread his arms wide. "Do I pass the decency test?"

"Yep. See you in a few."

With a wink, Wyld was out the door, leaving Micah alone with his thoughts. He dug out his phone and stared at the device. Micah hadn't turned it on since their first night on the East Coast. He hadn't considered calling or texting anyone since his last conversation with his dad. He couldn't even think about Detroit. Micah hadn't gone a day without talking to him since he was fourteen. Two months felt like an eternity. The betrayal cut deep.

The moment the device fired to life, a ton of texts rolled in. He wondered if his phone would ever stop chiming. When it finally fell silent, Micah immediately regretted opening his messages. They were all from his dad. Varying degrees of anger stared out at him. He'd have to face him again, eventually. It was best if it happened while Wyld wasn't around.

Before he could change his mind, Micah clicked on his dad's name and pressed the phone to his ear.

He answered on the first ring as if he'd snatched the phone up at the first sight of Micah's name. "I've been trying to call you for weeks."

"Hi, Dad."

The sound of air blowing across the phone came through the line as if his dad slowly released his breath. "Hi, Micah. Are you okay?"

"I'm good. I turned my phone off after I talked to you last. Guess I forgot to turn it back on."

A low laugh came through the phone. The sound made Micah smile. "You're the only person I know your age who isn't constantly glued to their phone. I bet you don't even have any apps."

Micah rubbed his chest, wishing it didn't hurt to hear his dad's voice. "Not true. There's one I use to check out books at the library."

His dad's voice turned serious. "I know I can't make you come home, but I wish you'd at least check in, so I know you're alive."

An ounce of guilt seeped in. It hadn't been his intention to make his dad worry. "If it makes you feel any better, I'll be back in a week."

"I guess it's a good thing I didn't set your stuff on the curb then."

Micah winced. He knew their peace was at an end. "I'll be back in town, but I'm not coming home. A guy named Cortland will come by in the next few days and pick up my stuff."

"To take it where?"

He could practically feel the muscle jumping in his dad's jaw. "To Wyld's."

"That's not happening." The response was so sharp and quick, Micah jumped like he expected to get slapped.

Still, he didn't back down. "I'm sorry, but it is. You've more than made it clear you don't like the idea of me being with Wyld, but since you don't know him, I don't understand why you're so set against this."

"I don't have to know him. His reputation is enough for any parent to balk. As to reasons, I have reasons. I have reasons for days. A, Wyld West is a well-known man whore. He won't be faithful to you. B, he's a terrible person who doesn't have a nice bone in his body. That's not the type person who could ever understand you or treat you how you deserve. C, you're my son and I won't have my son being kept as a billionaire's whore."

Micah eyed the giant teddy bear Wyld had given him as his dad ranted. Every single word melted Micah's heart, because even if they were true before Micah, they weren't true now. That meant Wyld was different for him. Micah was special to Wyld. He'd never been special to anyone.

"Are you even listening to me?"

"I'm listening." A soft chuckle escaped Micah. "It's just that you're wrong. About all of it. Since the first night I let Wyld take me to dinner and dancing, if he's looked at anyone else, I haven't seen it. He's also the best person I know. I've watched him fret over people losing their homes and businesses while plotting ways to help. As much as I love you and respect your opinions, you're just wrong about this."

Micah's voice grew stronger with each fact. Wyld was his, and no one would insult him. "Oh, and as to that last tidbit. Not only would I never let anyone treat me like a whore, Wyld wouldn't either. That's why he married me."

Dead silence met his confession. Micah checked the face of the phone, expecting his call had dropped. The timer still ran, so he pressed the phone to his ear. "Hello?"

His dad cleared his throat. "I'm not sure I heard you right."

Damn. He sounded deadly. "You did. It was a beautiful ceremony in the mountains. I'm sorry you weren't there, but I knew you wouldn't support me." Micah had to swallow his pain on those last words. When he spoke again, there was no missing his disappointment. "That's sad, actually."

Another bout of silence met his claims. When his dad finally spoke, he sounded resigned. "When Wyld destroys you, and he will, you'll always have a place with me." The phone beeped three times, letting him know his dad had hung up.

This time, Micah didn't bother turning off his phone. His dad wouldn't call again. He could only handle dealing with Micah when Micah did everything expected of him. The one thing his dad didn't tolerate was disobedience. Not from himself, his clients, and damn sure not from Micah.

The door swung open and Micah's unhappiness slipped away. Wyld stepped through the doorway carrying a thick envelope. He tossed it on a nearby table and focused on Micah.

"Longest ten minutes of my life," Wyld yelled as he ran from the door to the bed, before taking a flying leap onto the mattress. He tackled Micah to the bed, dragging peals of laughter from Micah. "I thought I'd never see my sexy husband's beautiful face again," Wyld cried, being as obnoxious as possible, and exactly what Micah's heart needed. While squishing him to the bed, Wyld placed several loud kisses all over Micah's face. Micah half-heartedly tried pushing him away. "Promise me you'll never let me out of your sight again. Swear it." Wyld's whine got louder and more screeched with each word. Micah could barely breathe from the laughter and the happiness choking him.

"Sometimes, I have to go to the bathroom," Micah finally choked out.

"No." The screech nearly burst Micah's eardrums. "I'll hold your hand if you do."

A loud snort escaped Micah. "You're not holding my hand in the bathroom."

"If you won't let me, I'll sit outside the door and whine like an abused dog and stick my fingers under the door like a little kid."

Micah couldn't stop laughing at the image Wyld painted with his claims. He was ridiculous enough to do everything he warned he would do.

Wyld settled down on top of Micah, stacking his hands on Micah's chest, and resting his chin on his hands. "Your happiness is the most beautiful sight in the world. Tell me how I can please you today."

Micah swiped his fingers through Wyld's hair. The belief he'd made the right decision by marrying Wyld grew stronger each day. He knew Wyld would do anything to make him happy. This man would never destroy him the way everyone claimed. Wyld deserved to have someone standing at his side, taking up for him. Micah would be that person. "Kiss me and I'll never be unhappy again."

"Damn right you won't," Wyld said, crawling higher.

The moment their lips met, Micah believed. In all his life, he'd never been surer about anyone or anything as he was Wyld and the power of his kisses. He knew everything would be okay. Wyld would never let his life be anything less than perfect.

EIGHT

WYLD DID NOT WANT to be here. With Micah running errands, gathering his books for the first semester and whatever else he would need, this was the only time Wyld could take care of this particular business. Unfortunately, the Den of Payne didn't accept phone calls. If he wanted to cancel his membership, he needed to do so in person, which meant finding Payne. The man's office was locked, forcing Wyld to visit the playroom. Jesus, all he wanted was to go home. He was entirely too sober for this mess.

A familiar looking dark-haired man met Wyld's gaze before Wyld could look away. His salacious grin said it all. Wyld cursed under his breath, but he wasn't quick enough to avoid the guy.

"Hey, sexy. You don't come around much anymore." He reached for Wyld as he made the claim.

Wyld didn't hesitate. He snagged the guy's hand before it touched him. "Sorry, Love. I'm not free."

"Wyld."

At the sound of his name being growled in a deadly tone, Wyld turned his head. Payne headed his way. A sigh caught in his throat. The last time someone had looked at him the way Payne did, inside this club, he'd been punched in the face. Sure enough, he found himself being hauled from the building the same as last time.

Sarcasm owned him as always. "Thanks for the offer, but I'm married."

Payne didn't slow on the way toward the exit. The door opened. Wyld went flying out, barely holding himself upright. "Your membership has been officially revoked."

Wyld blinked. "I seem to remember paying my bill." Confusion stopped him from pointing out he was there to cancel anyhow.

"You'll be reimbursed."

The hard set to Payne's jaw said he was serious. "I suspect I've done something, but damned if I recall what."

An evil light entered Payne's gaze. He looked deadly. "You broke the biggest membership rule of all. You married my son."

Wyld's brain didn't want to accept it. "At last count, I only have one husband, and I'm certain he's way too sweet and innocent to have ever been exposed to the likes of you."

An ugly sounding snort escaped Payne. "Micah is my son, idiot."

Well, fuck. Wyld refused to show an ounce of surprise. "That's..." Impossible came to mind, but there was something familiar about the way Payne held himself—like Micah did when he was standing his ground. Wyld's gaze moved over the man's features. His blond curls. "Damn."

"If you're showing up here, after marrying my son, you'd better have more to say than damn."

Wyld hadn't been forced to answer to anyone in years. He wasn't sure how to respond. "If you'd given me half a second, you would've known I came to cancel my membership. Your office was locked."

Payne's obvious outrage didn't lessen an ounce. "Please. Spare me. You haven't missed a day inside this club in years. I should've known you'd be back the moment you hit town. I tried warning Micah you'd ruin his life."

Payne's claim gave Wyld pause. He hadn't known Micah had informed anyone yet that they were married. "Wait. When did this happen?"

"When he called me a week ago."

Wyld had missed that, and Micah hadn't said a word. Obviously, Micah was free to call who he wanted, but he would've expected a conversation like that to upset Micah. Yet, he'd stayed silent.

Wyld swiped his hand through the air, wiping away his thoughts. What mattered now was what was in front of him. This was Micah's dad. They needed to get past this. "Why would you say something so spiteful to your son? He's happy, and I will make sure he stays that way."

"Don't fucking play the innocent son-in-law shit with me. Save it for someone who doesn't know you."

"You don't know me," Wyld said, getting angry despite his best efforts. "Seeing me inside your club isn't knowing me."

"Nothing from this place touches my son. This life is not his life."

Wyld couldn't respond because—fuck all—he agreed. This place wasn't for Micah. "It won't be," Wyld said, finally picking a response that didn't sound like he was being too agreeable. "As I said, I was here to cancel my membership. I apologize if you cannot accept that as the truth."

Payne's hate-filled expression never wavered. Wyld wasn't one to beg. He straightened his jacket and walked away. It looked like he now had a second family that he wouldn't be seeing on Christmas.

AFTER DUMPING HIS BOOKS AND SCHOOL supplies in the kitchen, Micah toed off his shoes. No sooner had he'd stashed them in the mud room than the doorbell chimed. A tired sounding sigh came from the depths of his soul. A loud booming knock followed the chiming, doubling Micah's irritation. He hated rude-ass people. He checked the security monitor as he passed. His steps faltered when he spotted his dad's image. For a moment, he considered not answering. In the end, he knew it was better to do this now while Wyld wasn't here to listen to the insults.

When the door swung wide, Micah hated himself for the hint of hope that filled him. He wanted to hug him. They hadn't gone this long without seeing each other since Micah was thirteen. "Dad."

Payne's face softened at Micah's greeting. "Hey Micah."

Micah took a step back, inviting Payne inside. He closed the door behind him. Micah fought the urge to fidget while waiting for his dad to say something.

Payne eyed the six-foot bear that Wyld had bought Micah during their trip to the mountains and the even bigger one that had arrived the day after they'd gotten home. Micah hadn't decided yet what to do with them. They were still hanging out in the foyer. Payne motioned toward the pair. "Dare I ask?"

A smile tugged at Micah's lips. "Gifts from Wyld. He doesn't do anything small."

His dad turned and met his gaze. "I just ran into Wyld. That's why I'm here."

A horrible feeling overcame Micah. His dad only went one place. "Is that so?"

"Yeah. I thought you'd like to know, I just kicked your so-called husband out of my club about an hour ago and revoked his membership."

It was like getting stabbed through the heart. Before Micah could think of a single response, the door opened. Wyld came pouring in along with the sun.

His gaze moved between Micah and his dad. "I'll leave you two alone."

"You," Micah snarled, surprising even himself with the growl in his voice. "Sit the fuck down." Wyld immediately sat in the closest chair by the door. Micah wasn't appeased. "I set one goddamn rule."

"And I've never broken it," Wyld said, sounding so calm and sure, it took most the wind from Micah's sails.

His anger was all he had. He'd been choking on it all his life. He focused on his dad. It came roaring back. His vision blurred. "How dare you show up here, trying to ruin my marriage? Why would you do such a thing? When did it become your goal to try to hurt me? First, Detroit and now this."

"Do I really have to sit through an argument about him stealing Detroit?"

Wyld's question gave Micah pause. "What the fuck are you talking about?"

"Please stop saying fuck, Angel. It just sounds wrong on your sweet lips. I'm talking about how you were in love with Detroit before you realized he was sleeping with your dad."

Micah's eyebrows pulled together in his confusion. "I was never in love with Detroit. Only an idiot would love Detroit. I'm talking about this one being party to Detroit pretending to be my friend, so they can be together."

"That's not how it happened," Payne argued, but no one was listening.

Wyld stood and waved his arms wildly. "Wait. You said at the park that you wanted Detroit, but he didn't want you."

For a moment, Micah was stricken mute by Wyld's blindness. "Are you kidding me right now? I never said Detroit's name. You assumed I meant Detroit when you asked who I wanted. I was talking about wanting *you*, stupid. Do you really think I'm the type person to fall in and out of love in the span of a day?"

The only thing saving Wyld from Micah's full rage was the way he shifted from foot to foot, as if all the pieces came together in his mind and he didn't know where to go with them. "No. You're not the type."

"Wait. Hold up," Payne said, inserting himself in the conversation. "You're in love with this guy?"

Micah was exhausted. He shook his head, trying to shake off the ignorance surrounding him. "Really? Why does everyone think I'm a fool? I would never, ever marry someone I don't love. Look...." Micah scrubbed his hands over his face. He hated confrontation. Micah focused on Wyld. "Do you think I married you for your money?"

Wyld didn't hesitate. "Not for one second."

Micah gave him a sharp nod and focused on his dad. "Do you think I'm capable of marrying someone for their money?"

Payne shook his head. "No. You're too much like your mom."

Micah's throat burned. He wanted to go back to living out of a suitcase with Wyld. Reality looked a bit bleak now that it was crashing down on him. When he spoke, his pain couldn't be hidden. His voice shook with it as he held his dad's stare. "I get that I'm just some kid you got stuck with, and you never really bonded with me." His gaze skirted away. It hurt too bad to look at the man he'd tried so hard to make love him. "So, this is me setting you free from having to run around behind me, cleaning up messes that don't exist. Go be with Detroit. I don't care. Just don't mess with Wyld again. Maybe he doesn't love me, but neither do you, so really, you should stop throwing stones." Once the words were out there, Micah just hurt. That was all. He couldn't take it. Without a word, he walked away. He didn't stop moving until the bedroom door closed and locked behind him. He was exhausted. Years and years of silence and trying too hard weighed on him. Now, all he wanted was to sleep. Life made him tired. He gave and gave, but no one ever loved him. No one ever would. Micah thought he'd accepted that. He thought he could live with it. Maybe he would try again later. Right now, depression owned him. He just wanted to stop existing for a little while.

WYLD STARED AT THE SPOT WHERE MICAH HAD been standing, furious and beyond sexy, only moments earlier. He couldn't think straight. All this time, he'd thought Detroit held a piece of Micah, but he hadn't. Now, Wyld was confused as hell.

"Say your piece too," Payne snapped, bringing Wyld back to the moment. His gaze swung the man's way. Payne looked ready to battle. His feet were braced, and his arms hung to his sides, like he could take any blow Wyld sent his way.

Wyld had nothing. "What the hell just happened?"

Payne's shoulders fell. "I just lost my son in a fight that's been a long time coming." Payne's huge chest expanded on a deep breath. "You should go after him. For some dumbass reason, he loves you, and he doesn't handle getting angry well. He'll need you."

Payne's claim knocked a bit of Wyld's shock from him. He straightened as his hackles went up. "Maybe, if you'd like to win your son back, you could start by not constantly referring to his every action as foolish, idiotic or dumbass. He's none of those things. Micah puts everyone first, even when it hurts him. In return, all he hears is how stupid he is for it." Aggravation raced through Wyld. Payne was right. Micah needed him. He needed to stop wasting precious seconds on someone who didn't see their faults. "Just get the fuck out," Wyld said, heading for the bedroom. He didn't bother looking to see if Payne complied. The man would stay or go. Either way, Wyld had an amazing husband who needed him.

The bedroom door was locked. Wyld sighed and followed the hall around through the living room and home gym until he found the other door to the room. He nearly sighed in relief when he found it unlocked. Wyld loathed the thought of kicking in his own bedroom door. Micah was sprawled across the bed, face down, and with his head buried beneath the pillows. He didn't budge even when Wyld climbed on the bed. Wyld didn't stop there. He straddled Micah's hips and placed several loud kisses on the side of Micah's neck.

Micah reached behind him and held the back of Wyld's head, keeping him in place for more kisses. "I'm sorry." The mumbled words enraged Wyld.

He refused to lose his temper. Not only was he not that guy who lost his shit, that was the last thing Micah needed. "Why are you sorry, Angel?"

"I don't know."

That's what Wyld thought. Micah was just apologizing to be apologizing. Going up onto his knees, Wyld urged Micah to turn over. "Roll over, babe." Wyld's heart squeezed at the first sight of Micah's face. He looked devastated and on the verge of falling apart. He swiped Micah's curls away from his face. "I have something I need to say, and I need you to listen. Are you listening?"

Micah nodded.

Wyld took a deep breath for courage. "I love you."

To his surprise, a tear rolled from the corner of Micah's eye. "Please don't toy with me right now. I can't deal with it today."

Wyld dropped his forehead to Micah's. "Angel, have I ever lied to you?"

Micah sniffed. "No."

"I'm sorry for not saying the words sooner. You might've noticed I'm not very good with baring my soul." Wyld sat back on his heels, unsure of where to start. "See, I'm from a family where people have children for stature. The minute I was old enough to be sent away to school, I was. The only time either of my parents showed any interest in me was when I pretended to care about property investment. Still, it was more about, 'look what I created' to my father than affection. No one in my family would ever lower themselves to loving anyone." Micah looked a little less miserable the more Wyld spoke, so he kept talking. "Then, I moved here. Everyone I met was the same. They all wanted what I could give them. I never cared because no one had ever loved me. Until you, I didn't think love existed. Yet, here you are. I knew almost immediately, you'd completely stolen me, but I'm not brave like you. Instead of throwing my heart out there, the way you did, I gave you tangible reasons to stay. Because, really, who could love me for me?"

Micah's hands lifted in a helpless gesture before falling back to the bed. He sniffed again. "Apparently, an idiot like me."

A growl rose in Wyld's throat and stuck. "That's

it. I have to take your car back. We had an agreement. You didn't punch your dad in the dick for talking down to you."

Micah didn't smile as Wyld hoped. "The first time I let you out of my sight, you went straight to a sex club. I don't think our deals mean that much to you."

"You mean everything to me." Even Wyld heard the seriousness in his voice, and he was rarely serious. He'd found humor and sarcasm always worked better for him. Not when it came to Micah. Micah was his world. "I spent the morning cancelling all my memberships at different places, because I'm yours. There's no way I could've known Payne is your father when I went there to cancel that one." Micah didn't stop him from rambling, so Wyld kept going. "For what it's worth, I've never touched your father. He's not my type. If someone's hurting me, it had better be because I'm getting paid. Not the other way around."

A loud groan escaped Micah. He covered his face with both hands. "Oh my god. Please be quiet. I never even thought of that."

Wyld's chuckle was out of his control. He snagged Micah's wrists and held them away from his face, leaving Micah no other choice but to look at him. "I love you, Micah West. Only you."

"Make love to me."

Wyld's brain stuttered to a stop at the demand. His mouth suddenly felt dry. He licked his lips. "Are you sure?"

Micah nodded. "I feel empty without you."

That was good enough for Wyld. He'd never let his angel feel empty. Wyld rolled from the bed and tugged Micah to his feet. He didn't rush. Instead, he stole several kisses as they stripped. Once nude, Wyld turned down the covers and urged Micah into bed. Micah's heated stare as he settled onto his back had Wyld sucking in a deep breath.

"You're the most beautiful man I've ever seen," Wyld said as he dug the lube from the bedside table. "I've been all over the world and no one has ever enchanted me. Only you."

Micah held his silence as Wyld crawled onto the bed. Wyld pressed a kiss to Micah's hipbone. He swiped his tongue across Micah's crown before moving to settle between his thighs. Still, Wyld didn't rush. He wanted Micah on the edge of madness.

"Can I tell you a secret?"

Micah's sweet smile made an appearance at the question. "Please? I want all your secrets."

Wyld rested his chin on his stacked hands on Micah's chest. As much as he wanted Micah, he didn't mind dragging out their moment all day. "I've dreamed of making love to you since the first day we met."

Micah laughed. His soft chuckle always made Wyld smile.

"That's not my secret," Wyld warned. "I've stroked myself with your name on my lips so many times. That's still not the secret."

Micah huffed.

Wyld was enjoying himself. "As long as I won your heart, I would've been happy for the rest of my life, even if you'd never let me touch you. Being in your company, that's everything to me."

"Awwww, is that the secret?"

Wyld shook his head. "When I called you the angel of miracles, what I really meant was you're my miracle." Wyld swallowed past the lump that jumped into his throat. "I'm still not convinced you're not a real angel," he added in a whisper. That was the only excuse Wyld could conceive for someone good like Micah ever taking a chance on someone like him.

Micah's expression turned understanding. He urged Wyld higher for a kiss. The moment their lips met, the slow burn inside Wyld became an inferno. Micah felt perfect beneath him. Wyld's hips moved of their own volition. He sucked Micah's bottom lip as his cock massaged Micah's. Micah gasped against his lips. The muscles in Wyld's stomach tightened at the sound. While playing with Micah's tongue, licking and sucking, Wyld fumbled with the lube. It took him longer than necessary since he refused to break their kiss. With his fingers coated, Wyld reached between them, making a huge mess. He spread lube over his cock before toying with Micah's asshole. The sounds Micah made drove Wyld insane. He needed inside Micah, but Micah wasn't ready. Wyld stroked Micah's erection. He pumped, trying to bring Micah to the edge of insanity. Wyld didn't let up until Micah's kiss turned desperate and he moved restlessly beneath Wyld.

Micah whimpered when Wyld stopped. It was like getting punched in the chest. Wyld needed to bring Micah release, but not yet. He wanted Micah crazed and uncaring of the pain as long as it ended in pleasure. Wyld toyed with Micah's asshole, stretching him with his fingers, and making room for his cock. Micah moaned. His fingers dug into Wyld's skin, urging him on.

Wyld eased inside. Sweat broke out on his skin as he fought to go slow. He pushed farther inside. Micah reached between them and tugged on his dick as if his patience was gone. Wyld pressed his forehead to Micah's chest and stared at the space between them. The sight of Micah pleasuring himself was his undoing. Wyld pushed, sliding inside to the hilt. The sexy sound Micah made ruined Wyld. He needed more. Wyld shifted positions, making it easier for Micah to jack off while he pumped inside him. Micah was so tight. Wyld knew he wouldn't last long. He was too turned on. All thoughts of going slow and being gentle fled. He needed what Micah's body offered—release. Micah visibly fought for air as his dick pumped inside his tight fist. Wyld pumped at an angle he knew would drive Micah insane. Micah's body tensed. Wyld gasped as Micah's already tight hole clamped down on his cock. Micah's orgasm hit. Wyld saw stars. Micah's asshole milked an orgasm from Wyld before he was ready. All Wyld could do was hold on and ride it out. He swore for a moment his eyesight went dim. Their lips met as they fought to get closer. A thousand vows ran through Wyld's head. One stood out above the rest. Micah would never regret him. Wyld wouldn't let him. As long as he lived, he'd ensure Micah woke up every day smiling and went to bed the same. For someone who had never believed in love, Wyld had found the greatest one of all. He wouldn't take it for granted.

NINE

EVEN THOUGH THE kitchen was nowhere near the bedroom, Micah still moved quietly, gathering his things and obviously thinking he'd sneak away while Wyld slept. Wyld leaned his shoulder against the doorframe and watched, waiting for Micah to notice him. When Micah finally turned, he dropped his phone and clasped his chest. Still, he didn't make a noise. He stared at the ceiling blinking until a hint of concern crept in.

"Are you having an attack?"

At Wyld's question, Micah finally dropped his chin. "I thought you were sleeping."

"I was until you left me alone and the bed didn't feel right anymore. Where are you going?"

"The mission. Saturday is my day to deliver meals."

"Do you care if I tag along?" Cortland asked, appearing from the back hallway and not looking their way.

Micah's smile was luminous. "Seriously? I'd love that."

Cortland cast a glance their way. "We've talked about how pants work, Wyld."

"My house," Wyld reminded him. His gaze slid Micah's way. "I mean, our house. Our rules."

Micah's eyebrows rose. "You're not covering what's mine," Micah said in a stage whisper.

Wyld smirked. "Let me go with you too and I promise to wear clothes."

Micah's expression made his impulsive offer worthwhile. He moved closer to Wyld, getting too close for Wyld's nudity while in Cortland's presence. "You want to go with me?" Damn, Micah looked so hopeful Wyld's chest tightened.

"There's no place I wouldn't go to be with you. I want to see what you do and be part of it. Plus, this is a good opportunity for us to look over the neighborhood and find the best place for this tiny home plan."

Micah flattened his palm against Wyld's chest

and backed him from the kitchen and out of Cortland's sight. His gaze never wavered from Wyld's, and his smile never fell. "I love you so much. You never stop wowing me."

There was nothing Wyld wouldn't do to keep Micah happy. Wyld stopped, refusing to budge until Micah moved closer. He snagged his sexy husband around the waist and hauled him against him. "Tell me you love me again, and I'll hurry."

"I love you more than the moon loves the sun."

That gave Wyld pause. His curiosity won. "Does the moon love the sun?"

Micah nodded, looking serious. "Why do you think they're always chasing each other?"

Wyld's mind stuttered to stop. "My god, I love you. That's the sweetest nonsensical thing I've ever heard."

A sexy laugh escaped Micah. He slapped Wyld's ass. "Get dressed so we can go. If we don't pick up our meals early, we'll be trying to find people all day."

Wyld backed away, watching Micah for as long as he could without falling over furniture. He covered his heart, acting ridiculous for Micah's smile. "My angel. Your beautiful smile is worth more than all the gold. I could give up oxygen as long as I have you."

Micah visibly took a breath. Wyld wondered if he was fighting an eye roll. "Get dressed, sexy."

With one last wink, Wyld turned away and headed for the bedroom. He couldn't wait to spend the day crawling through back alleys with Micah. There was nowhere else he'd rather be.

THEY'D BEEN WAITING IN THE ALLEY FOR fifteen minutes where he usually met Driver. Micah tried hiding it but worry ate at his gut. He'd been gone all summer. What if something happened?

"Have you seen Driver lately?" Micah asked, feeling panicked.

Cortland nodded. "Sometimes it took a little doing, but I always found him." Cortland pointed to a man-sized hole cut in the wire fencing at the back of the alleyway. "If you cut through there, there's a wooded area some ways back. He usually pitches a tent out there, but I don't advise going to look for him. I tried that once and his dog bit me."

Despite the news Cortland had been bitten by a

dog that possibly carried any number of diseases, Micah still smiled. "So, Sam is real?"

Cortland snorted. "Oh yeah."

Micah went back to chewing on his lip and worrying.

"This is the calmest I've seen Wyld in a long time. I'm glad he found you."

Micah cast a glance Wyld's way. He was literally trying to bounce from the walls between the fence and the brick buildings. A laugh caught in Micah's throat. He nodded Wyld's way. "This is the calmest you've seen him?"

Cortland didn't look. "Yes. He has ADHD and too much time on his hands. Wyld's also a self-medicater. Since he met you, he's been sober and looking for productive ways to stay busy. This is nothing. You should be proud."

Micah couldn't bite back his huge grin. Watching Wyld play was like standing in the sunshine. "He's amazing," Micah said without an ounce of shame for gushing over his husband. It was nice to talk to someone who wasn't bashing Wyld for once.

"He is," Cortland agreed, making Micah smile. "But not many people see it."

Cortland's praise had Micah's always ready to

overflow affection rising to the surface. "Wyld," he called, snagging the man's attention.

"My angel," Wyld called back without looking his way.

Micah didn't hold back. He didn't care what anyone thought. "I love you."

"I love you t..." Wyld's voice faded away as he looked Micah's way. His gaze locked on something over Micah's shoulder.

Micah turned. Detroit stood nearby—hands in his pockets and obviously waiting to be noticed. He looked like hell. Both his eyes were black and there was a deep gash across his nose.

"Jesus. What happened to you?" Micah moved Detroit's way without thought.

Detroit made a half-hearted effort to smile. He winced when the move obviously pulled at his split lip. "Hey, sweetie. How was your trip?"

Concern had Micah's chest hurting. He'd seen Detroit after losing a fight before. This was different. It was like his outer appearance was nothing compared to how he felt on the inside. His eyes looked haunted. Even though he wanted to ask, Micah stayed on topic. He held up his hand, showing off his ring. "It was amazing. I got married."

Detroit made another spiritless effort to smile.

"You've always been the both feet in type." Detroit's gaze shifted Wyld's way as Wyld flanked Micah's side. "I expect you to treat him right."

Micah's heart squeezed. He'd never seen Detroit so diminished.

"Only the best for my angel," Wyld said, sounding unusually serious.

Detroit nodded. His gaze moved back Micah's way. "Can I talk to you for a moment?" He focused on Wyld briefly. "Don't worry. I'm not here to talk him into leaving you or anything like that. There's some other shit I need to say."

Micah looked to Wyld for permission. He would do what he wanted, but if Wyld was uncomfortable with Micah talking to Detroit, he wouldn't do it.

Wyld shrugged. "Micah is free to have whatever friends he wants."

He made Micah proud. After squeezing Wyld's hand, Micah let Detroit lead him out of earshot.

"You look happy." Detroit looked everywhere but at Micah as he made the claim. "Who would've thought Wyld West would be the one who had the patience to win you?" he added as he leaned against the side of the building.

"He loves me." Micah realized he had no doubts as the words left his lips. Wyld did love him. He'd always known it in his heart. Wyld saying the words was nice, but he'd shown Micah how much he loved him from the very beginning.

Detroit's smile was sad. "You deserve it."

Micah touched Detroit's cheek, tilting his face toward the light so he could get a better look at the man's injuries. "What happened here?"

"It's nothing," Detroit said with a shake of his head. "I took a fight I didn't think I would win, and I was right." Detroit touched Micah's wrist, stroking once before gently moving Micah's hand from his face. He kept a light hold on Micah's hand. "I know you're the type person who lets things go without ever discussing them, but I still need to have my say, okay?"

Micah nodded, even though he really didn't want to discuss anything. Still, it wasn't fair to rob Detroit of having his say. "Okay."

"You're the only friend I have." Detroit blinked as he said the words as if they hurt. "I didn't mean to fuck that up, but that's what I do. The thing with Payne, that's the first time I felt like I couldn't talk to you. It seemed like the more I turned inside myself, the farther apart we drifted. That's not your fault. I wish things were different."

A lump formed in Micah's throat and wouldn't

budge. For everything he'd gained in the last few months, he'd lost just as much, if not more. He didn't know how to fix anything. "It might've been awkward, but you could've talked to me."

A sad smile passed over Detroit's features. "It would've been more than awkward. So much more. Not that it matters now. It's over. I'm sorry for everything. If I don't see you for a while, don't overdo it. You know how you like to take on too much and try to save everyone. Call me if you need anything."

Fear choked Micah. He didn't like Detroit's tone. "Why wouldn't I see you for a while?"

Detroit shrugged. "I'm moving to Vegas. Zander gave me permission to fight there. I think I need to get away from this place. There's nothing left for me here."

For the first time, Micah realized how unhappy Detroit was. He felt like the shittiest of friends for not noticing. "You can call me too. If you want."

A snort escaped Detroit. "You haven't answered a text or call from me in months."

"I blocked your number," Micah admitted with a wince. "I'll take the block off." He couldn't let the moment pass without speaking his mind. If Detroit never talked to him again, Micah knew he would regret any silence he held. "You're not alone. Whether you feel it or not, you still have me."

Detroit visibly swallowed. He looked everywhere but Micah's direction. "Don't worry over me. Just enjoy married life. This is the first time I've ever seen Wyld sober. That's something."

Micah glanced back at his husband. Wyld was moving his hands, talking in a very animated way to Cortland. Micah couldn't fight his smile. "Everyone keeps saying things like that. It's odd. I've only seen him not sober like twice, and we spend every minute together." He focused on Detroit once more.

Detroit's gaze was locked on Wyld. He chewed his bottom lip. "Maybe we're all just looking for that one person who keeps us high without the chemicals." He met Micah's stare. "See you around, babe."

"You too," Micah said around his rapidly swelling throat.

Detroit straightened away from the wall. "Okay, give me a hug and let me get out of your hair."

Micah didn't hesitate hugging Detroit back the second his giant arms encircled him. "Don't get all famous in Vegas and forget me."

"Who could forget you?" Detroit asked, pulling away. "You're too adorable."

"And you're still full of shit. Get lost," Micah said, slapping his ass as he started away. Detroit glanced over his shoulder. Micah fought the burning behind his eyes. They would never be friends again. He felt the invisible strings that had always kept them together being cut away. It was a lot harder than he could've imagined.

Wyld's body molded against his back, as Wyld drew Micah against his chest. He kissed the shell of Micah's ear. "Do you want me to chase him down and hobble him so he can't leave you?"

Micah tried for a smile and failed. "You hate Detroit and you know I bring home injured strays."

"You're right. I don't like him, but I love you."

Micah turned, giving up the final sight of Detroit to focus on his husband's gorgeous eyes. "He'll be okay, right?"

Wyld flashed him a patient smile. "I get the feeling Detroit always lands on his feet."

He was right. Detroit always seemed to come out on top. Micah cast a quick glance around. Cortland was gone. "Where did we lose Cortland?"

He felt Wyld shrug. "He decided to take Driver's food and risk losing a chunk of flesh to the man's rabid dog. Apparently, he knows exactly where the man stays."

Micah eyed the fence. "Should we go too? I'd hate for Cortland to get bit again?"

Wyld steered him toward the mouth of the alley where their SUV was parked nearby. "The last person you should ever worry about is Cortland. That's a man who can take care of himself. He was once homeless too, you know."

His steps faltered at Wyld's claim. "Are you joking? I didn't know."

Wyld kept his gaze locked on their destination and nodded. "When I first moved to the States thirteen years ago, I stumbled out of a bar at two a.m. barely able to stay upright. These guys followed me out and tried to rob me." Wyld paused for a moment as if an idea hit. "Well, at least I hope they were only trying to rob me. In truth, I was too messed up to remember much. Anyhow, Cortland slept in that alley. He saved me and kept me alive until I sobered up. I gave him a job, and he's been with me ever since."

Micah could only stare at Wyld as he opened the passenger side door for him. It was like Wyld was the perfect other half of him. The man always left him speechless. Micah started to climb in when he thought twice. "Wait. Are we leaving Cortland here?"

Wyld shrugged. "He said for us to go and he'd catch a cab home later. I learned not to argue with the man a long time ago." Wyld lowered his voice. His expression turned wicked. "I say we run home and fuck on the kitchen counter while he's away."

Even though Micah shook his head and laughed as if he found the suggestion ludicrous, he fully intended to do just that once they got home.

TEN

WITH MICAH BACK IN SCHOOL, sometimes it
was hard for Wyld to fill his day. Usually, he slept
most of the day, and then stayed up most of the night,
helping Micah study or playing with his angel. Wyld
couldn't control his smile at the thought. His lips
were permanently stretched into a grin these days.
He'd done a lot of crazy shit in his life and made
more mistakes than he could count, but marrying
Micah wasn't one of those things. They'd been
destined to meet in that back alley. Now, everything
was perfect. Well, except one thing. Micah still
wasn't speaking to Payne. Each time Micah's father
called, and Micah ignored him, Wyld saw the flash
of hurt Micah quickly hid. Wyld couldn't let this
continue.

With a walking stick in hand, to keep his nervous fingers busy, Wyld knocked on Payne's front door. He twirled the stick and eyed the house where Micah had once lived. It looked like a normal house on an ordinary street. The place was modest with yellow siding and a three-car garage. If Wyld had driven past the place, he would've pictured a four-person family with at least one child who played soccer. There was nothing about the house that told the real story—a sexual master lived beneath its roof.

The door swung open. Mismatched eyes—one blue and one green—stared out at him. If Payne was surprised to see him, he didn't show it. Of course, Payne Reynolds wasn't known for showing emotion. The man was all about discipline.

"Wyld."

"Payne," Wyld said back, keeping the same bland tone as Payne.

The man's odd gaze dropped to Wyld's toes and traveled up his body before landing on his face once more. "Do you ever wear a shirt?"

Wyld shrugged. "Only on occasion since I was twelve and my father almost succeeded in choking me to death with one." Even though Wyld kept the emotion from his voice, he'd given Payne more of his past than he gave anyone other than Micah.

Payne took a step back, silently inviting Wyld inside.

With a nod, Wyld stepped through the door. His gaze swung in every direction. The inside looked every bit as conventional as the outside. White walls. Leather furniture. Nothing special at all. "I expected this place to be..."

"Like a dungeon playroom," Payne supplied, sounding irritated.

Wyld snapped his fingers. "Yes. Like that."

"This is my home. Where I *was* raising my son," Payne said, putting an emphasis on was.

Wyld shrugged and continued pacing while inspecting photos on the shelves. "Your son is grown now. Into an amazing man, I might add." He kept his tone cordial because it wasn't his intention to fight. Micah loved his father. Whether Payne liked it or not, Micah was now married to Wyld. They needed to find a way past this bullshit for Micah's sake. Wyld stopped at a picture of a baby with huge eyes and blond curls. He lifted the frame. "Is this Micah?"

Payne nodded.

Wyld went back to staring at the image. "Adorable."

Payne moved to his side and plucked the frame from his hands. He stared down at the picture. "He wasn't supposed to be mine. Not really," Payne said, confusing the fuck out of Wyld. He set the frame back on the shelf and grabbed a different one before handing it to Wyld. It was a tiny baby. "That was the day he was born. Micah's mom, Kayla was my best friend. When she decided she wanted a baby, she asked me to be her donor. I didn't think it was a big deal. Micah was supposed to be hers alone. Then, he came into the world. I took one look at his big eyes and head full of curly hair and he was mine too. Kayla agreed to let me have visitation. Shortly after he turned thirteen, the area where she was working in Africa destabilized. She was too good hearted to leave, but it was too dangerous for Micah to stay. She sent him to me. I thought it would be hard, going from occasionally being a dad to a full-time parent. Not with Micah. He was so damn easy. As long as I picked my battles and let him care for every human stray he found, he never got in trouble. His grades were always good. Every damn time I look at him, I can't believe I helped create someone so amazingly beautiful. I guess I shouldn't be surprised he married a human stray."

Being as how Micah found Wyld in an alley, he couldn't bitch about Payne's description. Plus, he had been lost and adrift when Micah saved him. "No doubt you won't believe me, but I love Micah. As I've told him many times, it was never my intention to come between you two." Wyld set the picture back on the shelf. "It would nice if you could say the same of us."

Payne moved away and sat. "Micah is done with me, so it seems a moot point."

A snort escaped Wyld. "I don't think Micah is capable of truly being angry with anyone. Now, hurt, that's another story. My angel is hurting, and I can't have that." Wyld crossed the room and chose the seat across from Payne so he could hold the man's stare. "This conversation is about to get real uncomfortable for you, so buckle in," Wyld warned. "Since sexuality is your area of expertise, I'll break this down for you in a way that'll make sense to you. Your son is demisexual." He held up a hand. "Before you say, please god stop, and I don't want to hear this, let me explain why it matters. I don't think even Micah realizes there's a term for people like him or that he's not alone. Before me, the only person he'd ever confided in was Detroit, and let's face it, Detroit has never had an issue fucking anything that moves." Payne's blank expression didn't give away his thoughts. But his eyes said a million things. The depth of his betrayal was getting deeper.

"The first time I met Micah, he happily informed me that Detroit had been good enough to stay his friend, even though Detroit was sexy and athletic, while he is not. He was proud of keeping a friend who was never his friend because Detroit was here for you. The dirt in his wound was knowing he'd confided his most horrifying secret, a secret that made him feel like he wasn't as good as Detroit, to someone who was only here to fuck his father." Payne opened his mouth. Wyld held up his hand again, stopping him. "I know that's probably not the way of things. But I one hundred percent believe you were enjoying the wares. Despite that, I also think Detroit cares about Micah. I honestly believe Detroit thought of Micah as his best friend. No matter what the whole truth is, and no matter that we know there's absolutely nothing wrong with Micah, he feels how he feels. Now, you have to get the fuck over yourself and fix this, because—like I said—my angel is sad. That's not happening on my watch."

"He's right to be angry over Detroit. We shouldn't have kept our relationship a secret, but that's over. It's been over for a while."

"I know. We saw Detroit recently, or what's left of him."

A line appeared between Payne's eyes. "What's that supposed to mean?"

That wasn't the tone of someone who was over it. Because he couldn't stop himself from pushing people's buttons, Wyld shrugged as if it didn't matter. "It seems someone had beaten him senseless, but I'm sure he had it coming. Now, tell me how you plan to make things right with Micah."

Payne's hard expression fell away, making Wyld realize how much this was hurting him too. "I don't know how to fix this. This isn't the normal fuck up for me. I made too many mistakes at one time trying to keep him."

In Wyld's opinion, that was a brave confession coming from a control freak like Payne. "Lucky for you, I know how you can make it right. You'll have to over the top embrace me as your son-in-law."

Payne's groan said it all.

Wyld's smile felt evil, even to him. "Sorry, but you can't unfuck Detroit. That means you must accept me. Them's the rules."

"Jesus," Payne muttered. He sounded so much like Micah in that moment, Wyld had to stop himself from rubbing his chest. How many hours did he have left until Micah got home? He was ready to see his sexy husband now. "What do you want me to do?"

Smelling victory, Wyld stood. "Yes, Mr. Reynolds. Micah and I would love to join you at the Bronze Garden for dinner tonight at seven." He paused on his way to the door and met Payne's gaze. "Oh, and full disclosure, I won't be wearing a shirt. See you then." Without waiting for Payne to agree, Wyld let himself out. He whistled on the way to his car, refusing to let himself consider the possibility of anything going wrong. Payne might hate him, but that didn't make him unique, and Wyld could tolerate anything if it made Micah smile. Now, he just hoped Micah didn't punch him in the dick for setting up this dinner date from hell.

As much as Micah loved making Wyld smile, he hoped going out every night didn't become a habit. He was tired. For some reason his right arm ached, and he had test tomorrow. But Wyld had looked too excited about taking him to dinner for Micah to say no.

Thankfully, even though the restaurant required reservations, they didn't have a dress code. Micah wasn't up to putting on a tie. After being led to a table next to the window, Wyld squeezed in so close, Micah couldn't help but smile. It was hard to be in a bad mood around Wyld.

With his arm slung across the back of Micah's seat, Wyld placed several loud and wet kisses on Micah's cheek. He didn't stop until Micah laughed.

"Tell me what's wrong with my sexy angel," Wyld demanded, sounding like it mattered.

"Just tired. I know I need a college education, and it'll come in handy once we have all the tiny houses and the back-to-work program running. Right now, though, I'm exhausted with it."

Wyld nodded. His expression screamed understanding. Love overflowed inside Micah. "I want to point out that I could hire someone to run everything and you could just deliver meals or do whatever volunteering you want until your heart is content. But if you want a college degree for you, then I don't want to seem unsupportive. However, you don't need one if you're over it, because you never have to work." Wyld toyed with Micah's curls as he spoke. Micah's smile grew with each word. Wyld was adorable when he wanted to say what Micah wanted to hear but couldn't figure out what Micah wanted to hear. He loved this man.

Micah kissed the tip of his nose. "Thank you for being you."

"Sorry I'm late."

Micah's head snapped up at the sound of his dad's voice. He didn't look directly at Micah or Wyld as he pulled out a chair across from them and sat.

"Um." Micah had nothing.

Wyld caressed his thigh beneath the table. "Did I forget to mention your dad invited us to dinner?"

Micah stared at Wyld's guilt-ridden face and blinked.

"Guess so," Wyld added, sounding nervous.

"I didn't get to attend your wedding, so I thought I'd take the two of you out to celebrate."

Micah eyed his dad at the statement. He looked genuine. His shoulders relaxed a hair. If he was willing to accept Wyld, then Micah would let him try. "Thank you. We haven't been here long, so I don't think you're late."

Mismatched eyes turned his way. Micah swallowed his hurt. His dad nodded. "I've already talked to Wyld today, so I know how he's doing. How are you?"

The weight sitting on his chest was suffocating him, but Micah didn't think his dad wanted to hear that. Unfortunately, for some unknown reason, his throat wouldn't work to answer in any way.

"Micah's tired from school," Wyld answered for him. "You know the second year is the hardest. The shine of university has worn away, leaving you feeling as if it'll never end."

His dad continued watching Micah and nodding as if it was him speaking. "If you're unhappy, then you should quit. There's a lot of debate as to whether or not college helps or hurts. Not to mention, I'm sure Wyld doesn't expect you to work nor do you need to since you're married to him. Plus, it's my understanding he travels a lot. It'll be hard for you to take the time off you'll need to travel with him."

Micah weighed every word, looking for some fault or undertone. His dad sounded like he expected Micah and Wyld would be together forever. It was like the man had been taken over by an alien. The dad he knew would've lectured how Micah would need his education to get a good job once Wyld got bored and moved on. Micah didn't know how to react. So, he nodded and tried.

"That's true. Wyld just bought a bunch of land on the East Coast."

"We," Wyld said interrupting.

Micah glanced over. His face screwed up in confusion. "What?

Wyld flashed him a supportive smile. "We just bought a bunch of land."

Micah gave him a sharp nod. He knew how Wyld felt about everything being shared. "We just bought a bunch of land."

A worried look passed over his dad's face. "I hope that doesn't mean you plan to move."

Micah shook his head. "We have too much going on here. Wyld agreed to fund my idea to build a tiny homes community for the homeless and instill a back-to-work program. Once that's up and running, I'll be swamped here."

Payne sipped his water before responding. "I didn't know you wanted to do those things."

The spurt of irritation that kicked Micah in the gut obliterated his nervousness. "That's because you never talk to me about my volunteer work unless it's muttering under your breath how I'm an idiot who'll turn up dead in a back alley someday."

The way his dad stared at him—hardened— swelled Micah's throat. "That's because that's exactly what happened to your mom." That hurt. Payne kept talking. "She was my best friend, Micah. You're so much like her it hurts. I'm not like her or you. It doesn't bother me to know there are people out there who'd rather live in a tent than try to reach out for government help. I don't give a damn about anyone I pass on the street who's holding out a cup, begging for change. If they can stand there eight hours, they can stand in a factory for eight and get paid." He held up his hand, cutting off Micah's building outrage. "I know you don't feel the same, and I'm proud of who you are, but I can't take that call in the middle of the night twice in one lifetime. It pisses me off that Kayla cared more about strangers than she did about us. If anything happened to you, they'd have to dig a second hole for me, because I couldn't survive it." Micah's throat swelled, and his eyes burned, but his dad kept going, saying everything he'd obviously held onto for years. "She was my best friend," he repeated, as if Micah hadn't understood the first time. "Kayla was the only person who didn't think I'm a fucked-up, hopeless mess. I was happy to help when she wanted a baby because I loved the idea of sharing a part of her goodness. When I got that call, I'd never felt more betrayed in my life. I cannot tell you how I felt, knowing I would have to tell you that she chose the world over us. It's one thing to have your best friend betray you and know they're alive and you can fix it someday. I promise you it's a whole different experience to know they're dead and you'll never get to say how pissed off you are. So, no, you don't get to think for a second that I don't love you, because I would die for you. But it's hard for me to watch you constantly endanger yourself for people who don't even care about themselves." By the time he finished, Payne looked completely deflated.

Micah dropped his gaze to the table and stared at the white table cloth. He didn't know how to feel.

"This is going well. I can't wait to see what our holiday gatherings have in store." Despite Wyld's chipper tone, he kept rubbing Micah's thigh beneath the table, as if trying to comfort him.

Micah didn't know what to do next. He didn't think he should keep sitting there. "Maybe we should try again another night," he said to the table he couldn't stop looking at. "I'm not very hungry right now."

"Micah, look at me."

At his dad's order, Micah met his gaze. He looked broken-hearted. "I love you. There is no prouder parent on the planet." His gaze shifted Wyld's direction for a second. He sighed before meeting Micah's stare once more. "I can learn to love Wyld too, since it's obvious he loves you. Of course, only a stupid man wouldn't, but this is the one you chose, so I'll deal. Please stay and have dinner with me. I know I'm not very good at being a father, but I'm the one you got, and I don't want to lose you."

Micah nodded. He felt sick and not the least bit hungry, but he didn't want to leave. "I don't want to lose you either."

His dad's smile made the confession worthwhile. "Then, let's have dinner and see how it goes."

"Okay."

Wyld squeezed his thigh. Micah looked over at the man some would say he'd married recklessly. He was amazing. Micah didn't doubt for a second Wyld had been the mastermind behind all this. His husband never stopped plotting against the world. Micah didn't know if he could or would ever have a normal relationship with his father. After all, there was nothing normal about his family, but Micah knew—if they found their way—it was thanks to Wyld. Wyld glanced his way and winked. Happiness poured in, dousing the hurt. No matter what happened next, they would face it together. They were an unstoppable duo and would be forever.

PLEASE CONSIDER LEAVING A REVIEW AT THE retailer where this book was purchased. Reviews really help with a book's visibility, which ensures I can continue writing. Thank you, Charity.

KEEP AN EYE OUT FOR THE NEXT BOOK IN THE series, Sugar Dom.

ABOUT THE AUTHOR

Charity Parkerson is an award winning and multi-published author with several companies. Born with no filter from her brain to her mouth, she decided to take this odd quirk and insert it in her characters.

*Seven-time Readers' Favorite Award Winner
    *2015 Passionate Plume Award Finalist
    *2013 Reviewers' Choice Award Winner
    *2012 ARRA Finalist for Favorite Paranormal Romance
    *Five-time winner of The Mistress of the Darkpath

Connect with her online:

--Join my street team: facebook.com/TeamCharityParkerson
    --Sign up for my newsletter: http://bit.ly/CharityNews
    --Website: charityparkerson.com

--Facebook:

facebook.com/authorCharityParkerson

facebook.com/TheMenofSin

--Twitter: twitter.com/CharityParkerso